A NOTE TO TEACHERS AND PARENTS:

This collection is the most frightening book published in the Bal-Hi Series up to now. It is more frightening and powerful than collections of murder, war, and horror stories because its three authors, under the guise of exciting science fiction, create three specific prophecies which show what is happening to our civilization *today!*

Sometime, Never is in the tradition of Aldous Huxley's *Brave New World,* George Orwell's *1984,* and Ray Bradbury's *Fahrenheit 451* (Bal-Hi #U2843). But Golding, Wyndham, and Peake are more subtly frightening and intellectually stimulating in their horrible matter-of-factness than others of the same type.

Marshall McLuhan has pointed out that a good deal of science fiction being written today attempts to set up Utopian civilizations on Mars or Venus or Middle Earth by changing our sexual mores, or getting rid of the conventional ways in which the two sexes relate to one another and which we so take for granted. He sees this not as a gimmick of writers' imaginations, but as a profound criticism and prophecy of the direction that our society is indeed taking. The point is that stories about the future, the past, or of wild dreams (as these three are) are really ways of talking about the present. They are powerful criticisms of what we assume is a normal way of life. The authors, because they are trained artists, do not tell us (that would be lecturing and preaching), they show us, in dramatic action stories, what we are doing to ourselves.

The device used is *reductio ad absurdum*: to take a trait which most of us value and extrapolate it out to the next hundred or two hundred years, thus holding the mirror of natural cause and effect up to show us in the end how absurd we look. For instance, John Wyndham in "Consider Her Ways" takes the contemporary fact of the enormous popularity of women's magazines; the picture of ideal motherhood created in these magazines, in national advertising, and in television shows, and projects it to a time when men will have ceased to have any functional necessity in the world except to create wars and dominate. So they are dispensed with by women and the model for the full life is a fat, pink, illiterate woman who spends her life on a couch eating and every so often delivering four perfect babies who are, of course, raised by women to be mothers also.

William Golding does something even more frightening: he asks, in one of the most original stories he has ever written, if a powerfully wise emperor had been faced thousands of years ago with an inventor who could bring the world steam engines, explosives, and, above all, the printing press, what would the emperor do with such a man? In other words, what would you do, knowing all the good and all the bad that man's inventive curiosity has brought forth, if you were in the Garden of Eden again?

Wyndham and Golding write excitingly about where our technological developments and social institutions are taking us. Mervyn Peake's "Boy in Darkness" asks more upsetting questions. Not directly, but in the most hauntingly nightmarish, disturbing, and original story in this book, he asks what our modern mind, our personalities, and modern ideas of worship are doing to us. For some readers, this will be the most scathing satire on Christianity that science fiction has attempted. For others, it will be the most memorable creation of life on this planet after an H-bomb war, and for still others it will be the wisest descent into the blackness of man's soul where his deepest fears and perversions are hidden—even from himself.

This volume demonstrates that the appeal of great science fiction is not simply that it is highly imaginative and exciting, but that it contains some of the sharpest sexual, social, and political criticism that is being aimed at our way of life today.

RICHARD H. TYRE
CO-ORDINATOR OF HUMANITIES
ABINGTON HIGH SCHOOL
ABINGTON, PA.

Sometime, Never

three tales of imagination by

WILLIAM GOLDING
JOHN WYNDHAM
MERVYN PEAKE

Ballantine Books • New York

"Envoy Extraordinary" ©, 1956, by William Golding
"Consider Her Ways" ©, 1956 by John Beynon Harris
"Boy in Darkness" ©, 1956 by Mervyn Laurence Peake

Library of Congress Catalog No. 57-11580
Printed in the United States of America

PRINTING HISTORY
  FIRST PRINTING: JUNE, 1957
     Published: July, 1957
  SECOND PRINTING: SEPTEMBER, 1957
  THIRD PRINTING: NOVEMBER, 1962
  FOURTH PRINTING: NOVEMBER, 1971

Cover art by Gervasio Gallardo

BALLANTINE BOOKS, INC.
101 Fifth Avenue, New York, N. Y. 10003
An Intext Publisher

contents

The Past

ENVOY EXTRAORDINARY

by William Golding

THE TENTH WONDER

The curtains between the loggia and the rest of the villa were no defence against the eunuch's voice. His discourse on passion was understandably but divinely impersonal. It twisted and soared, it punched the third part of a tone suggestive of a whole man's agony, it broke into a controlled wobble, dived, panted neatly in syncopation for breath. The young man who stood against one of the pillars of the loggia continued to roll his head from side to side. There were furrows in his forehead as deep as youth could make them and his eyelids were not screwed up but lowered as if they were a weary and unendurable weight. Beyond and below him the garden was overwhelmed with sunset. A glow, impersonal as the eunuch voice, lay over him, but even so it was possible to see that he was exquisite to look at, tall, red-haired and gentle. His lips fluttered and a sigh came through them.

The old man who sat so restfully by the other pillar of the loggia looked up from his work.

"Mamillius."

Mamillius shrugged inside his toga but did not open his eyes. The old man watched him for a while. The expression on his face was difficult to read, for the sunlight was reflected from the stone pavement and lit him upside down so that the nose was blunted and an artificial benevolence lay about the mouth. There might have been a worried smile under it. He raised his voice a little.

"Let him sing again."

Three notes of a harp, tonic, sub-dominant, dominant, foundations of the universe. The voice rose and the sun continued to sink with remote and unimpassioned certainty. Mamillius winced, the old man gestured with his left hand and the voice ceased as if he had turned it off.

"Come! Tell me what is the matter."

Mamillius opened his eyes. He turned his head sideways and looked down at the gardens, level after declining level of lawn that yew, cypress and juniper shadowed and formalized, looked listlessly at the last level of all, the glittering sea.

"You would not understand."

The old man crossed his sandalled feet on the footstool and leaned back. He put the tips of his fingers together and an amethyst ring sparkled on one of them. The sunset dyed his toga more gorgeously than the Tyrians could manage and the broad, purple fringe looked black.

"Understanding is my business. After all, I am your grandfather, even though you are not from the main trunk of the imperial tree. Tell me what is the matter."

"Time."

The old man nodded gravely.

"Time slips through our fingers like water. We gape in astonishment to see how little is left."

Mamillius had shut his eyes, the furrows were back and he had begun to roll his head against the pillars again.

"Time stands still. There is eternity between a sleep and a sleep. I cannot endure the length of living."

The old man considered for a moment. He put one hand into a basket at his right, took out a paper, glanced at it and threw it into a basket on his left. Much work by many expert hands had gone to giving him the air of clean distinction he cut even before that garden and in that light. He was perfected by art, from the gleaming scalp under the scanty white hair to the tips of the tended toes.

"Millions of people must think that the Emperor's grandson—even one on the left hand side—is utterly happy."

"I have run through the sources of happiness."

The Emperor made a sudden noise that might have been the beginnings of a shout of laughter if it had not ended in a fit of coughing and a nose-blow in the Roman manner. He turned to his papers again.

"An hour ago you were going to help me with these petitions."

"That was before I had begun to read them. Does the whole world think of nothing but cadging favours?"

A nightingale flitted across the garden, came to rest in the dark side of a cypress and tried over a few notes.

"Write some more of your exquisite verses. I particularly

liked the ones to be inscribed on an eggshell. They appealed to the gastronome in me."

"I found someone had done it before. I shall not write again."

Then for a while they were silent, prepared to listen to the nightingale: but as if she were conscious of the too-distinguished audience she gave up and flew away.

Mamillius shook out his toga.

"Mourning Itys all these years. What passionate unintelligence!"

"Try the other arts."

"Declamation? Gastronomy?"

"You are too shy for the one and too young for the other."

"I thought you applauded my interest in cooking."

"You talk, Mamillius, but you do not understand. Gastronomy is not the pleasure of youth but the evocation of it."

"The Father of his Country is pleased to be obscure. And I am still bored."

"If you were not so wonderfully transparent I should prescribe senna."

"I am distressingly regular."

"A woman?"

"I hope I am more civilized than that."

This time the Emperor was unable to stop himself. He tried to untwist the laughter out of his face but it convulsed his body instead. He gave up and laughed till the tears jerked out of his eyes. The colour in his grandson's face deepened, caught up the sunset and passed it.

"Am I so funny?"

The Emperor wiped his cheeks.

"I am sorry. I wonder if you will understand that part of my exasperated affection for you is rooted in your very— Mamillius, you are so desperately up-to-date that you dare not enjoy yourself for fear of being thought old-fashioned. If you could only see the world through my regretful and fading eyes!"

"The trouble is, grandfather, I do not even want to. There is nothing new under the sun. Everything has been invented, everything has been written. Time has had a stop."

The Emperor tossed another paper into his basket.

"Have you ever heard of China?"

"No."

"I must have heard of China twenty years ago. An island, I thought, beyond India. Since then, odd fragments of information have filtered through to me. Do you know, Mamillius, China is an Empire bigger than our own?"

"That is nonsense. A contradiction in nature."

"But true, none the less. I sometimes fall into a daze of wonder as I imagine this ball of earth held, as it were, in two hands—one light brown and the other, according to my information, jaundice yellow. Perhaps at last man will be confronted with his long-lost twin as in that comedy."

"Travellers' tales."

"I try to prove to you how vast and wonderful life is."

"Do you suggest that I should go exploring?"

"You could not go by sea and it would take ten years by track or river if the Arimaspians would let you. Stay home and amuse an old man who grows lonely."

"Thank you for allowing me to be your fool."

"Boy," said the Emperor strongly, "go and get mixed up in a good bloody battle."

"I leave that sort of thing to your official heir. Posthumus is an insensitive bruiser. He can have all the battles he wants. Besides, a battle cheapens life and I find life cheap enough already."

"Then the Father of his Country can do nothing for his own grandson."

"I am tired of twiddling my fingers."

The Emperor looked at him more closely than the remark seemed to warrant. "Have I been very foolish? Be careful, Mamillius. A condition of our unusual friendship is that you keep your fingers out of hot water. Go on twiddling them. I want you to have that long life even if in the end you die of boredom. Do not become ambitious."

"I am not ambitious for power."

"Continue to convince Posthumus of that. Leave ruling to him. He likes it."

Mamillius looked at the curtains, took a step forward and murmured to the Emperor.

"Yet you would prefer that I should inherit the purple fringe on your toga!"

The Emperor leaned forward and answered him urgently.

"If his agents heard you we should neither of us live a year. Never say such a thing again. It is an order."

Mamillius returned to his pillar, while the Emperor took up another paper, held it in the sunset-glow and tossed it aside. For a time there was silence between them. The nightingale, assured of darkness and privacy, returned to the cypress and her song. The Emperor spoke softly at last.

"Go down the steps, cross the lawn that fills this coombe so neatly; pick your way past the lily-pond and enter the cliff-tunnel. After a hundred paces you will stand on the harbour quay—"

"I know the neighbourhood well enough."

"You will not be able to see much by the time you get there; but say to yourself, 'Here, shielded from the sea by the two quays are a hundred ships, a thousand houses, ten thousand people. And every one would give his ears to be the bastard but favourite grandson of the Emperor.'"

"Warehouses, taverns, brothels. Tar, oil, bilges, dung, sweat."

"You dislike humanity."

"And you?"

"I accept it."

"I avoid it."

"We must get Posthumus to allow you a governorship. Egypt?"

"Greece, if I must."

"Booked, I am afraid," said the Emperor regretfully. "There is even a waiting list."

"Egypt, then."

"A part of Egypt. If you go, Mamillius, it will be for your own sake. You would find nothing of me on your return but ashes and a monument or two. Be happy then, if only to cheer an ageing civil servant."

"What has Egypt to make me happy? There is nothing new, even out of Africa."

The Emperor unrolled another paper, glanced at it, smiled, then allowed himself to laugh.

"Here is something new for you. They are two of your prospective subjects. You had better see them."

Listlessly Mamillius accepted the paper, stood with his back to the Emperor and held it up to the light. He let go the end and glanced over his shoulder, grinning, as the paper rolled itself up. He turned and they laughed in each other's eyes. The Emperor laughed, enjoying himself, younger, delighted. Mamillius was suddenly younger, his laugh uncertain in pitch.

"He wants to play boats with Caesar."

So they laughed together under the song of the nightingale. The Emperor was the first to compose himself to stillness. He nodded towards the curtains. Mamillius went towards them, pulled one aside and spoke in a coldly formal voice.

"The Emperor will see the petitioners Phanocles and Euphrosyne."

Then he was back by the pillar and they were nodding and grinning at each other conspiratorially.

But Caesar could not be approached as though he were no more than a man. A fat secretary came through the curtains, sank on one knee and rested the tablets on the other. With a stamp and clank a soldier in full armour marched into the loggia. He came to attention behind the Emperor and a little to one side, rasped out a sword and flashed it upright. There were voices, whispering behind the curtain and two slaves drew them back. Someone struck a staff on stone paving.

"The Emperor permits you to approach him."

A man came through the curtain and a woman followed him carrying a burden. The slaves dropped the curtain and the man stood for a moment, perhaps dazzled by the sunset so that they had a moment or two to inspect him. He wore a light-coloured tunic and over that a long green cloak. His dark hair and beard were wild, ruffled either by the wind of his own approach or by some exterior insolence of weather that was not permitted to invade the Emperor's seclusion. The cloak was threadbare, patched and dusty. No one had taken care of his hands and feet. His face was lumpy, haphazard and to be accepted as nothing more than the front of a head.

The woman who had followed him shrank aside to the shadowy corner that seemed her natural place. She was little but a pillar of drapery, for a veil was over her head and caught loosely across her face. She stood sideways to the men and bowed her head over the bundle she carried. The instep lifted the long robe so that it revealed a sandal and four inches of modelled foot. The soldier made no sign behind his sword: only his eyes swivelling sideways raked her, assessing, expertly removing the wrappings, judging with the intuitive skill of long practice, from the few hints she allowed him, the woman who lay beneath. He saw a hand half-hidden, the rounded shape of a knee beneath the fabric. His eyes returned to their divided stare on either side of the sword. His lips pursed and rounded. Breathed through at a more propitious time and place they would have whistled.

Suspecting this transaction, the Emperor glanced quickly behind him. The soldier's eyes stared straight ahead. It was impossible to believe that they had ever moved or would ever move again. The Emperor glanced at Mamillius.

He was watching the woman sideways, his eyes, swivelling, raked her, removing the wrappings, judging with the intuitive and boundless optimism of youth the woman who lay beneath.

The Emperor leaned back happily. The man found his woman and took the bundle from her but could see nowhere to put it. He peered short-sightedly at the Emperor's footstool. The Emperor crooked a finger at the secretary.

"Take a note."

He watched Mamillius, kindly, triumphantly.

"Pyrrha's Pebbles, Jehovah's Spontaneous Creation, or the Red Clay of Thoth: but it has always appeared to me that some god found man on all fours, put a knee in the small of his back and jerked him upright. The sensualist relies on this. The wise man remembers it."

But Mamillius was not listening.

The wild man made up his mind. He removed some sacking from the bundle, bent and placed a model ship on the pavement between the Emperor and Mamillius. She was about a yard long and unhandsome. The Emperor glanced from her to the man.

"You are Phanocles?"

"Phanocles, Caesar, the son of Myron, an Alexandrian."

"Myron? You are librarian."

"I was, Caesar—an assistant—until—"

He gestured with extraordinary violence towards the boat. The Emperor continued to look at him.

"And you want to play boats with Caesar?"

He was able to keep the amusement out of his face but it crept into his voice. Phanocles turned in desperation to Mamillius but he was still occupied and more frankly now. Suddenly Phanocles burst into a flood of speech.

"There was obstruction, Caesar, from top to bottom. I was wasting my time, they said, and I was dabbling in black magic, they said, and they laughed. I am a poor man and when the last of my father's money—he left me a little you understand—not much—and I spent that—what are we to do, Caesar?"

The Emperor watched him, saying nothing. He could see that Phanocles had not been blinded by the sunset. The dregs of it were enough to show him that the man was short-sighted. The frustration of this gave him an air of bewilderment and anger as if some perpetual source of astonishment and outrage hung in the empty air a yard before his face.

"—and I knew if I could only reach Caesar—"

But there had been obstruction and more obstruction, mockery, incomprehension, anger, persecution.

"How much did it cost you to see me to-day?"

"Seven pieces of gold."

"That seems reasonable. I am not in Rome."

"It was all I had."

"Mamillius. See that Phanocles does not lose by his visit. Mamillius!"

"Caesar."

Shadows were creeping down from the roof of the loggia and welling out of the corners. The nightingale still sang from the tall cypress. The Emperor's eyes went like the soldier's to the veiled woman then, unlike his, to Mamillius.

"And your sister?"

"Euphrosyne, Caesar, a free woman and a virgin."

The Emperor allowed his palm to turn and his finger to crook until there lay on his lap the image of a beckoning hand. Drawn by that irresistible compulsion Euphrosyne moved noiselessly out of her corner and stood before him. The folds of her dress rearranged themselves, the veil fluttered over her mouth.

The Emperor glanced at Mamillius and said to himself:

"There is nothing new under the sun."

He turned to Euphrosyne.

"Lady, let us see your face."

Phanocles took a sudden step forward and found himself checked by the model.

He danced to save it from injury.

"Caesar—"

"You must accustom yourselves to our Western manners."

He glanced down at the sandalled toes, the moulded knee, up at the unbelievable hands clutched so tightly into the fabric of her dress. He nodded gently and put out the hand with the amethyst on it in assurance.

"We intend no discourtesy, lady. Modesty is the proper ornament of virginity. But let us see your eyes at least so that we may know to whom we speak."

Her head turned in the veil to her brother, but he was standing helplessly, hands clasped and mouth open. At last one hand drew down over her breast a little way and the veil came too so that it revealed the upper part of her face. She looked at the Emperor and then her head sank as though her whole body were a poppy stem and hardly strong enough for the weight.

The Emperor looked back at her eyes, smiling and frowning. He said nothing, but the unspoken news of his need had gone forth. The curtains parted and three women paced solemnly on to the loggia. Each seemed to carry a double handful of light in cupped hands so that faces were lit and the fingers a rose-coloured transparency. The Emperor, still watching Euphrosyne, began to arrange these nameless lamps with movements of a finger. One he beckoned to the right of her and forward, one behind her so that immediately the light ran and glittered in her hair. The third he moved in, close, close, bade the light rise till it was lifted by her face on the left side, so near that its warmth fluttered a curl by her ear.

The Emperor turned to Mamillius, who said nothing.

There was a shocked look on his face as though he had been jerked out of deep sleep. With a sudden motion Euphrosyne covered her face again and it was as though a fourth light had been extinguished. The soldier's sword was shaking.

The Emperor leaned back in his chair, and spoke to Phanocles.

"You bring the tenth wonder of the world with you."

The sweat was running down Phanocles' face. He looked at the model in bewildered relief.

"But I have not explained, Caesar—"

The Emperor waved his hand.

"Calm yourself. No harm is intended to you or your sister. Mamillius, they are our guests."

Mamillius let out his breath and looked at the Emperor. His head began to turn from side to side restlessly as though he were trying to break loose from invisible strings. Yet the Emperor's announcement had set another pattern in motion. The women ranged themselves to light the curtained doorway and the grave house dame came through it, willing to give of her plenteous store. She inclined her head to the Emperor, to Mamillius, to Euphrosyne, took her by the wrist and led her away. The curtains dropped together and the loggia was dark at last, the brightest lights were where the fishing boats danced by their nets. Mamillius came close to Phanocles and spoke to him in a voice that remembered how recently it had broken.

"What is her voice like? How does she speak?"

"She speaks very seldom, lord. I cannot remember the quality of her voice."

"Men have built temples for objects of less beauty."

"She is my sister!"

The Emperor stirred in his chair.

"If you are so poor, Phanocles, has it never occurred to you to make your fortune by a brilliant connection?"

Phanocles peered wildly round the loggia as though he were trapped.

"What woman would you have me marry, Caesar?"

Into the incredulous silence that followed his speech the nightingale spilled a rill of song. She had evoked the evening star that sparkled now in a patch of dense blue between the blacknesses of the junipers. Mamillius spoke in his rebroken voice.

"Has she an ambition, Phanocles?"

The Emperor laughed a little.

"A beautiful woman is her own ambition."

"She is all the reasons in the world for poetry."

"Corinthian is your style, Mamillius. However—continue."

"She is of epic simplicity."

"Your eternities of boredom will be sufficient for all twenty-four books."

"Don't laugh at me."

"I am not laughing. You have made me very happy. Phanocles—how did you preserve this phœnix?"

Phanocles was groping in a double darkness.

"What am I to say, Caesar? She is my sister. Her beauty has come up, as it were, overnight."

He paused, searching for words. They burst out of him.

"I do not understand you or any man. Why can they not let us be? Of what importance is the bedding of individuals? When there is such an ocean at our feet of eternal relationships to examine or confirm?"

They heard in the darkness a clucking sound from Phanocles' throat as though he were about to be sick. But when he spoke, the words were at once ordered and pointless.

"If you let a stone drop from your hand it will fall."

The Emperor's chair creaked.

"I hope we are following you."

"Each substance has affinities of an eternal and immutable nature with every other substance. A man who understands them—this lord here—"

"My grandson, the Lord Mamillius."

"Lord, do you know much of law?"

"I am a Roman."

Mamillius felt the wind of arms flung wide. He peered into the darkness of the loggia and made out a dark, gesticulating shape.

"There then! You can move easily in the world of law. I can move in the world of substance and force because I credit the universe with at least a lawyer's intelligence. Just as you, who know the law, could have your way with me since I do not, so I can have my way with the universe."

"Confused," said the Emperor. "Illogical and extremely hubristic. Tell me, Phanocles. When you talk like this do people ever tell you you are mad?"

Phanocles' bewildered face swam forward in the gloom. He sensed the model and hoped to avoid it. Then there was something before his face—a sword blade that glistened dully. He backed clumsily away.

The Emperor repeated the words as though he had not said them before.

"—tell you you are mad?"

"Yes, Caesar. That is why I—severed my connection with the library."

"I understand."

"Am I mad?"

"Let us hear further."

"The universe is a machine."

Mamillius stirred.

"Are you a magician?"

"There is no magic."

"Your sister is a living proof and epitome of magic."

"Then she is beyond Nature's legislation."

"That may well be. Is there any poetry in your universe?"

Phanocles turned, tormented, to the Emperor.

"That is how they all talk, Caesar. Poetry, magic, religion—"

The Emperor chuckled.

"Be careful, Greek. You are talking to the Pontifex Maximus."

Phanocles darted the shadow of a finger at his face.

"Does Caesar believe in the things that the Pontifex Maximus has to do?"

"I prefer not to answer that question."

"Lord Mamillius. Do you believe in your very heart that there is an unreasonable and unpredictable force of poetry outside your rolls of paper?"

"How dull your life must be!"

"Dull?"

He took a half-step towards the Emperor, remembered the sword and stopped in time.

"My life is passed in a condition of ravished astonishment."

The Emperor answered him patiently.

"Then a mere Emperor can do nothing for you. Diogenes was no happier than you in his tub. All I can do is to stand out of the sun."

"Yet I am destitute. Without your help I must starve. With it I can change the universe."

"Will you improve it?"

"He is mad, Caesar."

"Let him be, Mamillius. Phanocles, in my experience, changes are almost always for the worse. Yet I entertain you for my—for your sister's sake. Be brief. What do you want?"

There had been obstruction. The ship, not his sister, was the tenth wonder; he could not understand men, but with this ship the Emperor would be more famous than Alexander. Mamillius had ceased to listen and was muttering to himself, and beating time with his finger.

The Emperor said nothing as Phanocles rambled on, did nothing, but allowed a little cold air to form round him in the darkness and extend outwards. At last for all the man's insensitivity he faltered to a stop.

Mamillius spoke.

" 'The speechless eloquence of beauty—' "

"I have heard that before somewhere," said the Emperor thoughtfully. "Bion, I think, or is it Meleager?"

Phanocles cried out.

"Caesar!"

"Ah, yes. Your model. What do you want?"

"Let a light be brought."

One of the women returned with ritual solemnity to the loggia.

"What is your model called?"

"She has no name."

"A ship without a name? Find one, Mamillius."

"I do not care for her. *Amphitrite*."

Mamillius yawned elaborately.

"I think, grandfather, with your permission—"

The Emperor beamed up at him. "Ensure that our guests are comfortable."

Mamillius moved with a rush towards the curtain.

"Mamillius!"

"Caesar?"

"I am sorry that you are so bored."

Mamillius paused.

"Bored? Yes. I am. Sleep well, grandfather."

Mamillius strolled through the curtains with an air of leisurely indifference.

They heard how his steps quickened immediately he was out of sight. The Emperor laughed and looked down at the boat.

"She is unseaworthy, flat-bottomed, with little sheer and bows like a corn-barge. What are the ornaments? Have they a religious significance?"

"Hardly, Caesar."

"So you want to play boats with me? If I were not charmed with your innocence I should be displeased at your presumption."

"I have three toys for you, Caesar. This is only the first."

"I entertain you."

"Caesar. Have you ever seen water boiling in a pot?"

"I have."

"There is much steam evolved which escapes into the air. If the pot were closed what would happen?"

"The steam could not escape."

"The pot would burst. The force exerted by steam is titanic."

"Really!" said the Emperor with interest. "Have you ever seen a pot burst?"

Phanocles mastered himself.

"Beyond Syria there is a savage tribe. They inhabit a land full of natural oil and inflammable vapour. When they desire to cook they lead the vapour through pipes into stoves at the sides of their houses. The meat these natives eat is tough and must be cooked for a long time. They put one dish on top of another, inverted. Now the steam builds up a pressure under the pot that penetrates the meat and cooks it thoroughly and quickly."

"Will not the steam burst the pot?"

"There is the ingenuity of the device. If the pressure becomes too great it will lift the pot and allow the steam to escape. But do you not see? The upper lid is lifted—steam could lift a weight that an elephant would baulk at."

The Emperor was sitting upright, leaning forward, his hands on the arms of his chair.

"And the flavour, Phanocles! It will be confined! The whole wonderful intention of the comestible will be preserved by magic!"

He stood up and began to pace round the loggia.

"We should taste meat for the first time—"

"But—"

"I have always been a primitive where meat is concerned. Elephant's foot and mammoth, your rarities, spices, unguents, they are unworthy and vulgar. My grandson would plead that we should explore all variables and enlarge, as it were, the frontiers of gustatory experience—"

"My ship—"

"—but that is boy's talk. To taste meat in its exquisite simplicity would be a return to those experiences of youth that time has blunted. There should be a wood fire, a healthy tiredness in the limbs, and if possible a sense of peril. Then a robust red wine—"

They faced each other, two mouths open but for different reasons.

"Phanocles, we are on the verge of an immense discovery. What do the natives call their two dishes?"

"A pressure cooker."

"How soon could you make me one? Or perhaps if we simply inverted one dish over another—"

He was tapping one finger into the palm of the other hand, looking sideways at the garden but not seeing it.

"—or fish perhaps? Fowl? I think on the whole that fish would be preferable. One must find a little white wine of sufficient modesty to disclaim any self-pretension and sink itself wholly. Trout? Turbot? And at the same time of sufficient integrity to wait devotedly in attendance—"

He turned back to Phanocles.

"There is a southern vintage from that place in Sicily if I could remember the name—"

"Caesar!"

"You must dine with me now and we will formulate a plan of action. Yes, I dine very late. I find it gives me an appetite."

"But my boat, Caesar!"

"Amphitrite?"

Poised, ready to go, the Emperor waited.

"I could give you anything, Phanocles. What do you want?"

"When the wind falls what happens to a ship?"

Indulgently, the Emperor turned to him.

"She waits for the next one. The master invokes a wind. Sacrifices and so on."

"But if he does not believe in a wind god?"

"Then I suppose he does not get a wind."

"But if the wind fails at a moment of crisis for your warships?"

"The slaves row."

"And when they tire?"

"They are beaten."

"But if they become so tired that beating is useless?"

"Then they are thrown overboard. You have the Socratic method."

Phanocles allowed his hands to drop to his sides in a gesture of defeat. The Emperor smiled consolingly at him.

"You are tired and hungry. Have no fear for yourself or your sister. You have become very precious to me and your sister shall be my ward."

"I do not think of her."

The Emperor was puzzled.

"What do you want then?"

"I have tried to say. I want to build you a warship after the pattern of Amphitrite."

"A warship is a serious undertaking. I cannot treat you as though you were a qualified shipwright when you are only an ex-librarian."

"Then give me a hull—any hull. Give me an old corn-barge if you will, and sufficient money to convert her after this fashion."

"Of course, my dear Phanocles, anything you like. I will give the necessary orders."

"And my other inventions?"

"The pressure cooker?"

"No. The next one. I call it an explosive."

"Something that claps out? How strange! What is the third invention?"

"I will keep it in reserve to surprise you."

The Emperor nodded in relief.

"Do so. Make your ship and your clapper-outer. But first— the pressure cooker." Beaming, he reached out his hand, laid it gently on Phanocles' arm, turned him without force. And, compelled to follow by the first stirrings of courtiership, Phanocles kept in step, bowing a little towards the Emperor. The curtains swung open, released a flood of light that received and hid them. The light lay uninterruptedly on the secretary, the soldier, the empty chair; gleamed brightly from Amphitrite's brass boiler and funnel.

TALUS

Mamillius stepped down from the loggia to the garden. He was pleased with his appearance. The wide straw hat, enabling one to stand or walk in a pool of shade was sufficiently un-Roman to be a declaration of independence without being openly defiant. The light cloak, attached to either shoulder and cut from the thinnest Egyptian linen, added masculine dignity without oppression. If one walked fast—and for a moment he did so quite deliberately—it floated on the air and gave an effect of mercurial speed. The tunic was daringly short and slit at the sides but this, after all, was merely fashionable. If I were to come on her now, he thought, sitting between the lichened Naiads, would she not draw the veil from her face and speak? He kept his eyes open for her as he passed down the many steps, but the hot gardens were deserted. Each square of lawn was like velvet as it should have been according to literary convention and the clipped yew patterns were less alive than the statuary they surrounded. He peered into arbours and herb gardens, threaded his way between groups of stone Hamadryads, Fauns, Bronze Boys; he made the usual salutation mechanically before the Hermes that stood among the denser thickets.

But the trouble was she would not speak and was rarely to be seen. I know a little about love now, he thought, and not only from reading about it. Love is this nagging preoccupation, this feeling that the treasure of life has condensed itself to the little space wherever she is. I guess ahead and understand that love was reared in the wilderness and sucked the lion's dug. What does she think of me, how does she speak, is she in love?

A kind of burning spread over him and set his flesh trembling. I dislike this, he thought, I must not think of her. At that, a procession of horribly masculine lovers presented themselves to his imagination. By the time he had reached the lily-pond on the edge of the cliff at the foot of the garden he was struggling up out of his mind like a diver coming out of deep water.

"I wish I were bored again."

Perhaps the hat had not been such a good idea after all. The edges of his private pool of shadow were dulled and though the heat was already intense the sky to seaward was not as blue as it had been yesterday. There was a faint haze lying along the horizon and spreading towards the land. He spoke to a weather-beaten Satyr.

"We shall have thunder."

The Satyr continued to grin toothily. He knew what it was all about. Euphrosyne. Mamillius jerked himself away and turned to the left where the tunnel ran through the little headland and down to the harbour in the next cove. The sentry at the mouth of the tunnel came to attention. Partly because of the uninviting tunnel and partly because talking to soldiers always gave him a comfortable feeling of superiority, Mamillius spoke to him.

"Good morning. Are you comfortable here?"

"Sir."

"How many of you are there?"

"Twenty-five, sir. Five officers and twenty men, sir."

"Where are you billeted?"

The soldier jerked his head.

"Through the tunnel, sir. In the trireme alongside the quay."

"So I shall have to climb across her if I want to visit the new ship?"

"Sir."

"Tiresome. Pleasanter in the Emperor's garden than in the harbour, isn't it?"

The soldier thought.

"Quieter, sir. Very nice for them as likes a bit of quiet."

"You prefer your billets in hell?"

"Sir?"

Mamillius turned away and walked into the dark tunnel and a confusion of green after-images that remembered the toothy satyr. He held his breath for as long as possible because the guards used the tunnel as more than an approach to the gardens. The after-images were pierced and then replaced by his first view of hell.

To anyone but an Emperor's grandson in a brief and slit tunic, hell would have seemed an interesting and even attractive place. The port was built in a small bay that was like half a cup. Round it climbed gaudy warehouses and tenements that were painted red and yellow and white. The inside of the cup had a half-circle of quay running round it where every kind of vessel was lying, five or ten deep. The entrance to the cup was defended from the sea by two quays that almost met each other. The tunnel emerged on to the root of the nearer quay. Tenements, quays, warehouses, ships— they crawled with people. There were seamen, slaves or free, swinging over the sides of ships, and smearing on tar or paint. There were boys swung aloft and working at running rigging, there were men in skiffs and barges, and naked harbour rats oaring themselves after driftwood through the lolloping garbage. The hot air of the harbour shook the warehouses and tenements, shook the steep hills, would probably have shaken the sky if there had been any clouds to reveal the movement. Smoke from caulking braziers, from steaming pipes where the planks were twisted, from vats and cookshops and galleys dirtied the air and cast a hundred brazen shadows. The sun burned into all this and blazed from the water in the middle of the harbour in molten shapelessness.

Mamillius pulled down the brim of his straw hat and folded a corner of cloak across his nose. He paused for a while,

appalled and secretly gratified by his genuine distaste for
humanity and the violent mess they made of themselves.
Moreover he felt he had a contribution to make to the
mythology of hell. It not only stank and burned; it roared.
Noise climbed with the heat, vibration, a drum-roll of sound
on which screams floated like the twisted flight of a gull.

He turned from the port itself to the quay where his business was. The quay stretched across half the port to the
entrance with a shoulder-high wall to seaward. There were
three ships made fast to it. The first, on his left hand and only
a few yards from him, was the imperial barge. She lay low
in the water, her rowers sleeping on their benches in the
sun, a slave boy doing something to the cushions of her throne
under its huge purple baldachino. Ahead of her was the slim
shape of the trireme, her oars unshipped and stowed. Slaves
were working on her deck, but she was very dirty from the
traffic that crossed and recrossed her, for *Amphitrite* was made
fast on the outboard side of her, squat and uniquely ugly.

Mamillius strolled along the quay as slowly as possible,
putting off the moment when he would have to endure the
heat from her hold. He stopped by Phanocles' second invention and examined it curiously, for he had not seen it before.
The tormentum had been set up and trained over the wall,
pointing out to sea. Against all military sense, Phanocles had
wound back the chain that served for a string and cocked the
mechanism. Even the sledge that would drive the peg and
release the string was lying ready. There was a bolt lying in
the groove and on the other end of the bolt was a shining
keg ending in a brass butterfly with a projecting iron sting. The
thing was a suitable insect for hell. Strike the peg and the bolt
would buzz seaward, out to the fishing boats, would bear the
keg to them, a drink with the Emperor's compliments.

Mamillius shuddered at the machine, then laughed as he
remembered Phanocles' explanation. In the end, desperately,
as though the Emperor were a child, he had flung out his
arms, said one sentence and refused to add to it.

"I have shut lightning in the key and can release it when
I will."

The sentry who had been dozing behind the tormentum
found himself discovered and attempted to cover his fault by

chatting as though he and Mamillius were on one side of a fence and military discipline on the other.

"Nice little horror, isn't she, sir?"

Mamillius nodded without speaking. The sentry looked up at the heat haze creeping over the quay wall.

"Going to have thunder, sir."

Mamillius made the sign that averts evil and walked hastily along the quay. There was no sentry on the trireme to meet him and no one to greet him at the gangway. Now that he was aboard her he could identify the ground bass to the uproar of the harbour—the slaves in every ship were growling like beasts that lust for the food of the arena. The only silent slaves were those working listlessly, moodily on deck. He crossed the trireme amidships and stood looking down at *Amphitrite*.

She made the tormentum look like a toy. Projecting from her on either side were the biggest wheels in the world and each wheel bore a dozen paddles. A great bar of iron that Phanocles had had twisted into a wicked shape writhed its way across the deck between them. Four metal hands held this bar, two pushing, two pulling back. Behind the hands were iron forearms and upper arms that slid back into sleeves of brass. Mamillius knew what Phanocles called the sleeves. They were the pistons; and because there was no other way of making them with the ludicrous accuracy he demanded they had been drawn off two alabaster pillars that had been intended for a temple of the Graces.

Reminded by the Graces of Euphrosyne, Mamillius turned aft. Between the pistons was the most daunting thing of all: Talus, the man of brass. He was headless, a flashing sphere half-sunk in the deck, his four arms reached forward and gripped the wicked crank. Between him and the crank, fitting in the space that the arms left between them was a brass funnel, tall as a mast, scandalous parody of the Holy Phallus.

There were few men about. A slave was doing something highly technical to one of the steering paddles and someone was shovelling coal in the hold. The coal grit lay everywhere on her deck and sides and paddles. Only Talus was clean, waist deep in the deck, breathing steam, heat, and glistening with oil. Once *Amphitrite* had been a corn-barge that labourers had hauled up the river to Rome, an ungainly box, smelling of chaff and old wood, comfortable and harmless. But now she was possessed. Talus sat in her, the insect pointed over the harbour wall and hell roared.

Phanocles poked his head out of the hold. He squinted at Mamillius through his sweat, shook his beard and wiped his face with a piece of waste.

"We are almost ready."

"You know the Emperor is coming?"

Phanocles nodded. Mamillius grimaced at the coal dust.

"Haven't you made any preparations for him?"

"He said there was to be no ceremony."

"But *Amphitrite* is filthily dirty!"

Phanocles peered down at the deck.

"This coal costs a fortune."

Mamillius stepped aboard gingerly.

"The hottest corner in hell."

The heat hit him from the boiler and sweat streamed down his face. Phanocles looked round at Talus for a moment then handed Mamillius the piece of waste. He conceded the point.

"I suppose it is hotter than usual."

Mamillius waved away the waste and wiped his streaming face on the corner of his elegant cloak. Now that he was cheek by jowl with Talus he could see more of his construction. Just above deck level at the after-end of the sphere was a projection surrounded with springs. Phanocles, following his gaze, reached out and flicked the brass with his fingers so that it tinged and gave out a puff of steam. He looked moodily at the projection.

"See that? I call it a safety valve. I gave exact instructions—"

But the craftsman had added a winged Boreas who touched the brass with an accidental toe and rounded his cheeks to eject a fair wind. Mamillius smiled with constraint.

"Very pretty."

The springs strained, steam shot out and Mamillius leapt back. Phanocles rubbed his hands.

"Now we are ready."

He came sweatily close to Mamillius.

"I have had her out in the centre of the harbour and once

out in the bay. She worked as certainly and easily as the stars."

Mamillius, averting his face, found himself regarding his own distorted face in Talus' shining side. It faded away from the mouth and pointed nose. No matter how he moved it followed him with the incurious but remorseless stare of a fish. The heat from the boiler and the smoking funnel was like a blow.

"I want to get out of this—"

He made his way under the contorted cranks and paused in the bows. The air was a little cooler here so that he took off his straw hat and fanned himself with it. Phanocles walked forward too and they leaned their backs against the bulwarks. Slaves were working on the fo'castle of the trireme only a few feet above them.

"This is an evil ship."

Phanocles finished wiping his hands and dropped the waste over the side. They turned to watch it drift. Phanocles pointed upward with his thumb.

"She is not evil. Only useful. Would you sooner do that?"

Mamillius glanced up at the slaves. They were clustered round the metal crab and he could see most of it though the claws were hidden by the trireme's deck.

"I don't understand you."

"Presently they will centre the yard-arm and swing the crab up—all ten tons of it. Steam would do it for them without fuss or exertion."

"I do not have to swing the crab up. I am not a slave."

They were silent for a while, standing on tip-toe to inspect the crab. It was a spreadeagled mass of lead and iron, its claws resting on blocks of stone to keep them from cutting through the deck. It was as strictly utilitarian a mass as could have been found anywhere in the Empire, for its sole use was to be dropped through an enemy's bilges and sink her outright: but the same impulse that had made the brass on the keg into a butterfly and stood a Boreas on the safety valve had been at work on the crab too. The makers had indicated the eyes and the joints of the legs. It had a kind of formal significance and the slaves were tending it—cleaning the claws—as if it were more than metal. Other slaves were swinging the seventy-foot yard round, were centring the hoist over the ring.

Mamillius turned and looked along *Amphitrite's* deck.

. "Life is a perplexing muddle, Phanocles."

"I shall clean it up."

"Meanwhile you are making it dirtier."

"No slaves, no armies."

"What is wrong with slaves and armies? You might as well say, 'No eating or drinking or making love'."

For a while again they were silent, listening to the roar of the port and the shouted orders from the trireme.

"Ease her down. Handsomely!"

"This evening the Emperor is going to try your pressure cooker. The one you made for him."

"He will forget all that when he tries *Amphitrite*."

Mamillius squinted up at the sun. It was not so bright, but he still fanned himself.

"Lord Mamillius—has he forgiven us for the improvised cooker?"

"I think so."

"Sway back. Take the strain. Walk. One, two. One, two."

"And, after all, without that experiment I should have never known that a safety valve was necessary."

"He said that a mammoth was too much to begin with. Blamed me."

"Still?"

Mamillius shook his head.

"All the same, he is sorry about the three cooks and the north wing of the villa."

Phanocles nodded, sweating. He frowned at a memory.

"Do you think that was what he meant by a 'Sense if possible of peril'?"

The slave who had been firing the furnace climbed to the deck and they watched him idly. He threw a bucket over the side on a rope's end, hauled up water and tipped it over his naked body. The water flowed along the deck, carrying snakes of coal dust. Again and again he laved the filthy harbour water over himself. Phanocles called to him.

"Clean the deck here."

The slave touched his smeared forelock. He drew up another bucketful, then shot it along the deck so that water splashed over their feet. They started up with a shout of annoyance and there came the sound of a rope breaking under strain. *Amphitrite* ducked under them, sidled and made a loud wooden remark as though she had crunched one of her own timbers with metal teeth. There came a dull thump from the harbour bottom, then a huge cascade of water fell on them from the sky, water full of garbage and mud and oil and tar. Phanocles stumbled forward and Mamillius bowed under the torrent, too shocked even to curse. The water ceased to fall from the sky but surged, waist-deep, over the decks instead. Puffs of steam spurted from Talus like ejaculations of rage. Then the water had all streamed away, the decks were shining and the roar of the harbour had risen to a frenzy. Mamillius was cursing at last under a hat like a cow pat and in clothes that clung greasily to him. Then he was silent, turning to the place where they had leaned and talked. The crab had snatched away six feet of the bulwarks, had torn off planking from the deck and laid bare the splintered beam ends. The huge cable led straight down from the yard of the trireme into the water where yellow mud still stank and swirled. A mob of men were brawling on the trireme, and soldiers were among them, using the pommels of their swords. A man broke free. He stumbled to the quay, seized a loose stone, clasped it to his stomach and plunged over the harbour wall into the sea. The struggle sorted itself out. Two of the Emperor's guards were bashing heads impartially.

Mamillius went white slowly under the filth that covered him.

"That is the first time anyone has tried to kill me."

Phanocles was gaping at the broken bulwarks. Mamillius began to shiver.

"I have harmed no one."

The captain of the trireme came, leaping nimbly to the deck.

"Lord, what can I say?"

The frenzy from the harbour seemed as though it would never die away. There was the sense of eyes, thousands of eyes watching across the deceptive embroidery of the water. Mamillius gazed wildly round into the white air. His nerves were jerking. Phanocles spoke in a foolishly complaining voice.

"They have damaged her."

"Curse your filthy ship—"

"Lord. The slave who cut the cable has drowned himself. We are trying to find the ringleader."

Mamillius cried out.

"Oloito!"

Use of a literary word was a safety valve. He shivered no more but began to weep instead. Phanocles put his shaking hands close to his face and examined them as though they might have information of value.

"Accidents happen. Only the other day a plank missed me by inches. We are still alive."

The captain saluted.

"With your permission, lord."

He leapt back aboard the trireme. Mamillius turned a streaming face to Phanocles.

"Why have I enemies? I wish I were dead."

All at once it seemed to him that nothing was safe or certain but the mysterious beauty of Euphrosyne.

"Phanocles—give me your sister."

Phanocles took his hands from his face.

"We are free people, lord."

"I mean, to marry her."

Phanocles cried out in his thick voice.

"This is too much! A plank, a crab—and now this—!"

Hell closed in on Mamillius, haze-white and roaring. Somewhere in the sky the thunder grumbled.

"I cannot bear life without her."

Phanocles muttered, his eyes on Talus.

"You have not even seen her face. And you are grandson to the Emperor."

"He will do anything I want."

Phanocles glanced sideways at him, savagely.

"How old are you, lord? Is it eighteen or seventeen?"

"I am a man."

Phanocles made a pattern of his face that was intended for a sneer.

"Officially."

Mamillius set his teeth.

"I am sorry for my tears. I have been shaken."

He hiccuped loudly.

"Am I forgiven?"

Phanocles looked him over.

"What do you want with my forgiveness?"

"Euphrosyne."

All at once Mamillius was trembling again. Beautiful shoots of life sprouted in him. But Phanocles was frowning.

"I cannot, explain, lord."

"Say no more now. We shall speak to the Emperor. He will persuade you."

There came the crash of a salute from the mouth of the tunnel.

The Emperor was walking briskly for his age. His crier went before him.

"Way for the Emperor!"

There was a guard and several veiled women with him. Mamillius began to rush round the deck in a panic, but the women detached themselves from the group of men and ranged themselves by the harbour wall. Phanocles shaded his eyes.

"He has brought her to watch the demonstration."

The captain of the trireme was hurrying along by the Emperor, explaining as he went, and the Emperor was nodding his silver head pensively. He mounted the gangway to the trireme, crossed her deck and looked down at the strange ship before him. Even in these surroundings his spare figure in the white, purple-fringed toga cut a shape of clean distinction. He declined a helping hand and stepped down to *Amphitrite's* deck.

"Don't try to tell me about the crab, Mamillius. The captain has told me all about it. I congratulate you on your escape. You too, Phanocles, of course. We shall have to abandon the demonstration."

"Caesar!"

"You see, Phanocles, I shall not be at the villa this evening. I will examine your pressure cooker another time."

Phanocles' mouth was open again.

"In fact," said the Emperor agreeably, "we shall be at sea in *Amphitrite*."

"Caesar."

"Stay with me, Mamillius. I have news for you."

He paused and cocked his ear critically at the harbour noises.

"I am not popular."

Mamillius shook again.

"Neither am I. They tried to kill me."

The Emperor smiled grimly.

"It was not the slaves, Mamillius. I have received a report from Illyria."

A look of appalled understanding appeared beneath the mud on Mamillius' face.

"Posthumus?"

"He has broken off his campaign. He has concentrated his army on the seaport and is stripping the coast of every ship from triremes to fishing boats."

Mamillius made a quick and aimless step that nearly took him into the arms of Talus.

"He is tired of heroics."

The Emperor came close and laid a finger delicately on his grandson's sodden tunic.

"No, Mamillius. He has heard that the Emperor's grandson is becoming interested in ships and weapons of war. He fears your influence and he is a realist. Perhaps our unfortunate conversation on the loggia reached the ears of the ill-disposed. We dare not waste a moment."

He turned to Phanocles.

"You will have to share our council. How fast can *Amphitrite* take us to Illyria?"

"Twice as fast as your triremes, Caesar."

"Mamillius, we are going together. I to convince him that I am still Emperor, you to convince him that you do not want to be one."

"But that will be dangerous!"

"Would you sooner stay and have your throat cut? I do not think Posthumus would allow you to commit suicide."

"And you?"

"Thank you, Mamillius. Amid all my worries I am touched. Let us start."

Phanocles pressed his fists to his forehead. The Emperor nodded to the quay and a procession of slaves began to cross the trireme with luggage. A little Syrian came hurrying from aft. He spoke quickly to Mamillius.

"Lord, it is impossible. There is nowhere for the Emperor to sleep. And look at the sky!"

There was no longer any blue to be seen. The sun was dispersed into a great patch of light that might soon be hidden completely.

"—and how am I to hold a course, lord, when I can no longer see the sky and there is no wind?"

"It is an order. Grandfather, let us get ashore for a moment at least."

"Why?"

"She is so dirty—"

"So are you, Mamillius. You stink."

The Syrian sidled up to the Emperor.

"If it is an order, Caesar, I will do my best. But first let us move the ship outside the harbour. You can transfer to her from your barge."

"It shall be so."

They crossed the trireme together. Mamillius ran to the tunnel with head averted from the women and disappeared. The Emperor went to where his barge was moored astern of the trireme and arranged himself comfortably under the baldachino. It was only then that he began to realize how ugly and preposterous the new ship was.

He shook his head gently.

"I am a very reluctant innovator."

The crowd of slaves aboard *Amphitrite* was being absorbed by her hold and the small crew was busily casting off. The crewmen of the trireme were bearing off with the looms of oars and she began to move sideways. Her cables splashed free in the water and were hauled aboard. The Emperor, under his shady purple, could see how the helmsman was heaving at the steering oars to bring her stern in and give her bows a sheer away from the trireme. Steam was jetting constantly from the brass belly over the furnace. Then he saw Phanocles stick his head out of the hold and wave the helmsman into stillness. He shouted something down to the bowels of the machine, the jet of steam increased till the scream of it rasped the air like a file then suddenly disappeared altogether. In answer a snarling roar rose from the ships and houses round the harbour till *Amphitrite* lay like some impossible lizard at bay in the centre of an arena.

The Emperor fanned himself with one hand.

"I have always considered a mob to be thoroughly predictable."

There came a grunt from the bowels of the ship and an iron clank. Talus moved all four hands, two back, two forward. Both wheels began to revolve slowly, port astern, starboard ahead. The blades of the paddles came down—smack, pause, smack!—so that dirty water shot from under them. They rose out of the water, throwing it high in the air, to fall back on the deck. The whole ship was streaming and steam rose in a cloud again, but this time from the hot surface of the sphere and the funnel. A great wailing came from her hold and Phanocles leapt on deck, to stand there, inspecting the deluge through screwed-up eyes as though he had never seen anything so interesting. *Amphitrite* was lying in one place, making no way, but turning; and the water sprayed up as from a fountain. Phanocles shouted down the hatch, the steam jetted up, the paddles creaked to a stop, and the water was running off her as though she had just come up from the bottom of the harbour. The noise from the people stormed at her as she lay in the centre of harbour with her steam jet screaming. There was a blink of light in the haze over the hills and almost immediately the thud of thunder.

The Emperor made a furtive sign with two fingers.

The lightning, however, was a divine irrelevance. As the Emperor shielded his eyes in expectation of *Amphitrite's* destruction at the hands of an outraged Providence he glimpsed that she was not the only portent moving on the waters. Outside the harbour mouth but visible over the quay wall there was a solidity in the moving vapours. Before his mind had time to work he thought of it as the top of a rock or a low cliff. But the rock lengthened.

The Emperor scrambled ashore, crossed the quay and climbed the steps of the harbour wall where the women were sitting. The rock was clear of the mist. It was the prow and fo'castle of a great warship and from her hold came the measured beating of a drum. She was slightly off course for the entrance of the harbour but swinging already to bisect the narrow strip of water that lay between the two quays. Steadily she came on, sail furled on the yard, a crab suspended at either yard-arm, ejaculatory armament trained forrard, her decks glistening with steel and brass, the twenty-foot spear of her ram cutting the surface of the water like a shark. The drum tapped out a change of rhythm. The centipedal oars closed in aft as though they had been folded by a central intelligence. She slid through the entrance and her ram was in the harbour. The drums changed rhythm again. Pair after pair as they were free of the obstructing quays the oars unfolded, reversed, backed water. The Emperor saw a red and gold banner on the quarterdeck surmounted by a vindictive-looking eagle. He dropped down from the harbour wall, ignored the questions of the women and hurried back to his barge and the shelter of the baldachino.

Aboard *Amphitrite* they had noticed the warship too. The Emperor saw Phanocles and the captain gesticulating fiercely at each other. Phanocles ducked down the hatch, the jet of steam vanished and the paddles began to move. Immediately the captain ran along the deck, there was a flash of steel and *Amphitrite*'s anchor thumped into the water. But the drums were beating out another order. The oars of the warship rose and were rigid like spread wings. She glided forward with the last of her momentum like a vast and settling seabird. Her ram took *Amphitrite* under the starboard paddle and tore it. Men were swarming along the horizontal oars, leaping down, striking with sword hilts and the butts of spears. The growl of the harbour rose to a frantic cheer. Phanocles and the captain were hauled up between the oars and dumped on the warship's deck. Her oars began to move again so that the ram slid out of the torn wheel. *Amphitrite*, her wheels turning very slowly, began to revolve round her own anchor. The warship, starboard oars paddling ahead, port astern, was moving towards the quay where the trireme and the Emperor was.

The Emperor sat, pulling on his underlip. There were more moving cliffs outside the harbour, warships backing and filling, waiting to come in. There was another blink of light and clap of thunder but this time the Emperor did not notice it. Mamillius was standing on the quay by the barge in the

attitude of one arrested at a moment of extreme haste. The
Emperor, glancing sideways, was transfixed also.

Mamillius was dressed in armour. His breastplate flashed
from a multitudinous and highly allegorical assembly of heroes
and centaurs. A scarlet cloak dropped down his back to his
heels. The red leather of his sword scabbard matched exactly
the red leather openwork of the boots that reached nearly
to his knees. The breastplate was matched in material and
complexity by the brass helmet that he carried under his
left arm.

The Emperor closed his eyes for a moment and spoke
faintly.

"Bellona's bridegroom."

Mamillius seemed to collapse a little. He blushed.

"I thought—as we were going to the army—"

The Emperor surveyed the details of the uniform.

"I see that both Troy and Carthage have fallen."

The blush came and went, came again with a profuse
perspiration.

"I thought—I liked—"

"Do you know whose warships these are?"

"I—"

The Emperor rested his forehead on one hand.

"In the circumstances, a distaff would have been less open
to misconstruction."

Always Mamillius kept the wall of his cloak between him
and the women. He saw the gold and scarlet banner shake as
the warship came alongside the trireme. Her ram lay alongside
the barge. This time the colour left his face and did not
return.

"What shall we do?"

"There is no time to do anything. Perhaps you might put
your helmet on."

"It gives me a headache."

"Diplomacy," said the Emperor. "He has the soldiers—
look at them! But we have the intelligence. It will be hard
if we cannot smooth things over."

"What about me?"

"On the whole, I think you would be safer in China."

The Emperor took Mamillius' hand and stepped ashore.

He walked along the quay towards the warship with Mamillius at his heels. The crowd from her deck had flooded the trireme and was flowing across the quay so that the end by the harbour entrance was jammed full. There were prisoners, the abject and supplicating Syrian, slaves. Phanocles wearing an even wilder air of short-sighted bewilderment and soldiers, far too many soldiers. They bore huge bundles and bags that made them look as though they were about to contribute to a gigantic jumble sale. They were tricked out in favours of red and yellow. The loot of a countryside was suspended about them but they came to attention under their loads when they saw the purple fringe on the white toga. The Emperor stopped by the gangway and waited. Behind him the women were crouched by the harbour wall, veiled and terrified like a chorus of Trojan Women. Someone blew a large brass instrument on the warship, there was a clash of arms and the banner was dipped. A tall, dark figure, burly, armed and flashing, and full of intention, came striding down the gangway.

"Welcome home, Posthumus," said the Emperor, smiling. "You have saved us the trouble of coming to see you."

JOVE'S OWN BOLT

Posthumus paused for a moment. His gold and scarlet plume waved a foot and a half above the Emperor's head. His olive-dark and broadly handsome face took on a look of calculation.

"Where have you hidden your troops?"

The Emperor raised his eyebrows.

"There are a few sentries in the garden as usual and possibly a few by the tunnel. Really, Posthumus, you travel with a considerable retinue."

Posthumus turned aside and spoke briefly among his officers. A detachment of laden legionaires doubled along the quay and stationed themselves between the Emperor and escape. The women wailed then settled to a steady lament. The Emperor affected not to notice but drew Posthumus towards the barge. *Amphitrite* continued to circle round her anchor slowly.

Posthumus stopped.

"It was high time I came home."

More thunder. The Emperor looked back at the dense mass of soldiers that filled the end of the quay.

"About a hundred men, I should say. An Imperial Salute?" Posthumus snorted.

"You can call it that. Presently more ships will enter the harbour. There will be sufficient to ensure that we agree on all points of policy. But what a stroke of luck to find you both on the quay!"

Mamillius cleared his throat and spoke in a high uncertain voice.

"Posthumus, you are mistaken."

"Mamillius in arms."

"For show only. I do not want to be Emperor."

"Ah!"

Posthumus took a step towards him and Mamillius started back, tripping on his cloak. Posthumus poked a finger in his face.

"You may think not. But he would bridge the Adriatic to please you."

The Emperor flushed a delicate pink.

"You have never wanted my affection, Posthumus, so you have never missed it. If I have been foolish enough to think that I could enjoy his company without more danger than the usual scandal, I have been wise enough to know that you are the best man to rule the Empire—however uncongenial I may find you."

"I am informed otherwise."

"At least you might gloss over our differences in public."

Posthumus paid no attention to these words, but fished a folded paper from inside his breastplate.

"To:
    Posthumus, etc., Heir Designate, etc.
    From:
    CIII
    Ships and weapons are being built or converted on the quay next to the tunnel. The Emperor and the Lord Mamillius take much personal interest in a ship, *Amphitrite*, ex-corn-barge, unclassified, and a tormentum (mark VII)

that has been placed on the quay and trained seaward. They are also experimenting with methods of poisoning food on a large scale. Lord Mamillius seems to be in a state of high excitement and anticipation—"

"Posthumus, I swear—"

Posthumus merely raised his voice.

"He is corresponding with the Emperor and others in code under cover of writing poetry—"

Mamillius was flaming.

"Leave my poetry alone!"

"It has not yet been found possible to break this code. Submitted to XLVI; it proved to be composed of quotations from Moschus, Erinna, Mimnermus, and sources not yet identified. Research is proceeding."

Tears of rage ran down Mamillius' face.

"You filthy swine!"

"That was unnecessarily cruel, Posthumus."

Posthumus stuffed the paper back.

"Now we have done with fooling, Caesar. The time has come for a regency."

"He does not want to be Emperor."

Posthumus sneered at Mamillius.

"He is not going to be."

A faint clattering sound came from Mamillius' armour. The Emperor laid a hand on Posthumus' arm.

"If the ship and the tormentum worry you, Posthumus, I can explain them rationally. Be fair."

He turned to the officers and raised his voice.

"Bring the Greek to me."

Posthumus nodded, waiting. Phanocles stood before them, restoring the circulation to his wrists.

"This man is the root of the matter."

"Lord Posthumus—I am altering the shape of the world."

"He has this curious manner of speech, Posthumus."

"There will be no slaves but coal and iron. The ends of the earth will be joined together."

Posthumus laughed and the sound cheered no one.

"And men will fly."

He turned to the officers and beckoned.

"Colonel—why aren't those ships coming in?"

"Visibility, sir."

"Damn the visibility. Signal them in or send a message."
He turned back to Phanocles.

"This fantastic ship—"

Phanocles spread his arms.

"She will go faster than any other. Civilization is a matter
of communications." He frowned at them and searched for
simple words. "Lord Posthumus. You are a soldier. What is
your greatest difficulty?"

"I have none."

"But if you had?"

"Getting there first."

"You see? Even warfare is a matter of communications.
Think of the elaborate efforts Xerxes made to conquer Greece.
With *Amphitrite* he could have crossed the Aegean in a day
and against the wind."

Mamillius struck in, teeth chattering, eager to help.

"Think of the first Caesar, of Alexander, Rameses—"

Phanocles sank his head on one side and opened his hands
as if the explanation was simple.

"You see, lord? Communications."

The Emperor nodded thoughtfully.

"They should be made as difficult as possible."

Thunder rumbled again. Posthumus strode over to the tormentum and the women shrank away. The roar of the harbour
was rising again.

"And this?"

"I have shut the lightning in the keg. The sting when it
strikes anything looses the lightning. Then there is a smoking
hole in the ground."

The Emperor made a sign with two fingers.

"What is the brass butterfly at the base of the sting?"

"It is an arming vane. After the keg has gone some way
the butterfly shoots off, otherwise the keg would explode by
set-back when you fired the tormentum."

"Would this make a smoking hole where there was a city
wall?"

"Yes, Caesar."

"Where there was an army?"

"If I make the keg big enough."

Posthumus considered Phanocles closely.

"And this is the only one you have made?"

"Yes, lord."

"I am not sure whether to have you executed straight away or use you for other purposes."

"—Execute me?"

Suddenly the roar from the harbour rose till it could no longer be ignored.

They turned together.

It was *Amphitrite*; they understood that immediately. She had revolved endlessly round her anchor till her flaunted eccentricity had become more than any man could bear who had red blood in his veins. There were naked men plunging from ships and jetties till a hundred arms flashed in the water.

Phanocles cried out.

"What—?"

Posthumus spoke rapidly to the Colonel.

"All troops will disembark on this quay. Meanwhile neither the Emperor nor his suite will wish to leave. See that his wishes are respected. You understand?"

"Sir."

Posthumus ran to the barge but the Emperor called to him.

"While I am waiting I will inspect these splendid fellows already assembled."

The Colonel glanced at Posthumus, who laughed softly.

"Do as the Father of his Country tells you."

The arc of swimmers converged on *Amphitrite* and the second warship was coming in to the sound of drums. Phanocles clasped his hands.

"Stop them, Caesar!"

Men were swarming now over *Amphitrite*, tearing at her paddle, striking with any heavy gear they could find at the brass monster in the deck. The guard that Posthumus had put aboard her went down in a whirl of limbs. Smoke rose suddenly from her hold and uncoiled. Naked figures were hurling themselves from her bulwarks while a thin flame, hooded and flickering like a ghost, shot up amidships. The second warship saw the danger and backed water. Oars smashed against the quay but her way was checked. A third ship, emerging from the heat haze crashed into the second with her ram. More oars smashed; then both ships were locked and drifting helplessly down on *Amphitrite*. Posthumus, screaming curses, leapt into the imperial barge.

"Bear off there! Give way!"

"Detachment ready for inspection, Caesar."

"Those men between me and the tunnel, Colonel. Let them join the others."

"My orders, Caesar—"

"Do you not think, Colonel, that you could catch half a dozen women and one old man if they tried to escape?"

The Colonel swallowed.

"This may be the last time the Father of his Country will inspect his troops. Will you not obey, Colonel? I am a soldier too."

The Colonel's Adam's apple went up and down twice. He swelled with understanding and emotion. He flashed the Emperor an enormous salute.

"Detail to join parade at the double!"

"And the band," added the Emperor. "I think I see the band there. The band, Colonel?"

A fourth warship was gliding into the harbour. *Amphitrite* lay, her brass boiler nested in smoke and flame. Her paddle wheels began to lumber round faster. She strained at her cable. They heard a wild scream from Posthumus.

"Back water, curse you!"

Flutes, buccinas, tubas. The brass tube of each *lituus* was wound round the waist and projected in an elephantine bell over the shoulder. Drums, kettle and bass. Scarlet and gold.

The parade filled the end of the jetty and faced the trireme. The band formed up between the parade and the tormentum. The women wrung their hands. *Amphitrite* was revolving and flailing up flames and smoke. The fourth warship was trying to circle round her and the other two. But a fifth was about to enter the harbour.

"Band!"

Amphitrite was moving faster. A fathom or two of her cable eased out and she fetched a wider circle, brushed the locked warships so that their rigging flamed. Posthumus was jumping up and down.

"Use your crabs!"

Amphitrite veered another fathom or two of cable. Her circle included the imperial barge which got under way with extraordinary lack of ceremony. Round she went, round and round, with Posthumus screaming and *Amphitrite* breathing fire down her neck.

The band struck up.

"Open order, Colonel?"

The Colonel quivered.

"There is no room, Caesar. They would step straight down between the quay and the trireme."

"In that case," said the Emperor, "they will have to carry their impedimenta and loot or I shall not be able to walk between the ranks."

The band began to countermarch between the main detachment and the tormentum, ten paces forward, ten paces back. They were splendid. The men were splendid. The seamen were splendid aboard their utterly splendid ships. The women felt the men were splendid and that if they themselves were in danger from General Posthumus it was worth it. Chests swelled, bosoms heaved, and calves quivered. Mamillius put his helmet on.

The Emperor paused by the left-hand man of the first rank.

"And how long have you been in the army, my man?"

Amphitrite's cable charred through and snapped. Her turning circle became a wide sweep. She touched one of the trots of merchantmen moored by the warehouses and immediately they were dressed overall with flame.

"Somebody use a crab!"

All at once every man in every ship was possessed by one idea—to get out of the harbour. A burning warship limped astern past the end of the quay and the heat from her scorched the parade. Outside *Amphitrite's* dreadful arc the water was hidden by ships great and small that fought each other and strove for the safety of the haze-covered sea. Over all this the thunder rolled, dropping bright light into the hills; and the band played.

"Where did you get that scar? A jab with a spear? A bottle, eh?"

The legionaries stood rigidly to attention under their sixty-four pounds of brass, their impedimenta, their loot, and the dreadful heat. The Colonel watched a drop of sweat forming on the tip of his nose till his eyes crossed. The Emperor spoke to each man in the front rank.

There was a mess of warships revolving in the centre of the harbour with *Amphitrite* nuzzling them. The captain of one of them was facing Posthumus at the salute. At that moment either a cable charred through or someone, in blind obedience, used a crab. A black star-shaped hole appeared on the quarterdeck where the captain had been. He went down with his ship.

"How tall are you? Do you like the army? Where did you get that dint from? A slingstone? I should have said a slingstone, shouldn't you, Colonel? Don't ever let the Quartermaster issue you with a new shield, my man. Tell him the Emperor said so. How many children have you got? None? We must arrange some leave after this inspection."

The word 'leave' spread. The legionaries stiffened to endure but already some of them were swaying. The Emperor moved along the front rank with awful deliberation.

"Don't I remember you from the IXth? In Greece? Why haven't you been promoted? Look into that, Colonel, will you?"

A second warship was extracting herself from the harbour among a mass of smaller shipping. *Amphitrite* was bearing down on the harbour mouth in pursuit of the Emperor's barge.

"What are you going to have done for that boil, my man? Here's what I call a really impressive fellow. How on earth he can support those three bundles I don't know. What's your name?"

Suddenly there was a gap of air in front of the Emperor and a brazen crash. The legionary had passed out.

"As I was saying, we must arrange some leave for them now that the Heir has brought them home to their Father."

"Caesar—"

"Where did you lose that eye, my man? Don't lose the other, will you?"

Crash.

Oil was spilling from a warehouse and burning on the water. A thick cloud of black smoke drifted across the parade.

The Emperor spoke softly to the Colonel.

"You see how comedy and tragedy are mingled. Whose orders will you take? These men ought to be putting out the fires."

The Colonel's eyes uncrossed for a moment.

"I have my orders, Caesar."

"Very well. Now, my man, how do you like the army? Has it made a man of you?"

Crash.

"Discipline," said the Emperor to the right-hand man, "is a great convenience."

"Caesar?"

"I should have said a splendid thing of course."

He stood looking down into the sooty water of the harbour entrance. A constant flow of singed traffic was passing before him. The band drowned the language that came from it, but judging from the contorted faces it was complex and personal. *Amphitrite* and the imperial barge came through almost together.

"Tell me, sergeant, if I gave the orders 'Right turn, quick march' would you obey me?"

But the sergeant was an old soldier, mahogany-coloured and indestructible. His loot was worth all the rest on the quay, but it was in a tiny bag suspended under his breast-plate. Even so the sweat ran off him.

"In the 'oggin, armour an' all, Caesar?" For a moment the disciplined eyes flickered sideways and down. "I'd be glad to."

It was not only the smoke and sweat that threw up a meditative gleam in the Emperor's eye.

"Sir! Caesar!"

The words burst from the Colonel. His sword was vibrating and the veins in his neck were swelling like ivy-branches. The Emperor smiled peacefully and turned to worm his way between the ranks. It was like being in a tunnel under the huge bundles, in the thick air and before the row of bulging eyes. But there were a number of air-holes already where

Posthumus' chosen men lay flat on their backs, keeled over on
parade. The little trail of men, the Colonel, Mamillius,
Phanocles, wormed after the Emperor. The panic uproar of
the town, the harbour and the shipping was punctuated by
the brazen fall of legionaries.

Outside the harbour the warships were disappearing into
the heat haze and all the small ships were trying to get back
in. *Amphitrite* was moving more slowly. As the heat built up
round her boiler she would make a clumsy advance between
her flailing paddles. But the paddles threw up so much water
that this movement damped down the fire again and she
would slow to a stop. So she wove a complex and unpredictable pattern over the water in a series of clownish lunges. She
was settling low in the water.

The band continued to play.

Crash. Crash. Crash.

March and counter-march, worm between the thinning
ranks. The Watch on the Rhine, Entry of the Gladiators,
Guardians of the Wall, the Old Cth, excerpts from The
Burning of Rome and The Boys We Left Behind Us. The
tenements were on fire, their washing flaming like the rigging of ships. In the warehouses wine burnt brightly but
corn only smouldered and stank.

"And now," said the Emperor, "I will address them." He
climbed the harbour wall and stood for a moment fanning
himself. "Will you turn them about, Colonel?"

The band fell in, the town burned, *Amphitrite* sank, hissing.
The townspeople were outward bound for the open country.
It was a scene of godlike and impersonal destruction.

Crash.

"—have watched you with growing pride. You evince in
these decadent modern times the spirit that made Rome
great. Yours not to reason why, yours but to obey your
master's voice."

Mamillius, standing at the foot of the wall, could see the
shadows of the Emperor and the Colonel on the quay at his
feet. One of them was swaying gently backwards and forwards.

"Under the weight of the sun, the joyous oppression of
sixty-four pounds of brass, bearing on your shoulders the
heavy fruits of your labours you have stood and endured be-

cause you were ordered to. This is what we expect of our soldiers."

Mamillius began to work his feet heel and toe as he had learned to do as a child. He looked straight before him but moved smoothly and unnoticeably away from the inspection. Soon the women and the sheltering bulk of the tormentum hid him.

"Ships burned before your eyes. A town was laid waste by pitiless fire. Reason told you to put the flames out. The common and undisciplined dictates of humanity whispered to you that women and children, the aged and the sick required your assistance. But you are soldiers and you had your orders. I congratulate Rome on her children."

Mamillius had vanished. The women were disposed in a graceful group between the parade and the tunnel. The Colonel found he could see nothing but two swords that drifted further and further apart. He put his left hand cautiously under his right wrist to steady them.

The Emperor reminded the troops of Roman history.

Romulus and Remus.

Crash.

Manlius, Horatius. The Standard Bearer of the IXth.

Crash.

The Emperor traced the expansion of the Empire, the manly virtues which they so admirably exemplified. He outlined the history of Greece, its decadence; touched on Egyptian sloth.

Crash. Crash.

Suddenly the Colonel was no longer at his side on the seawall. There came one loud plop from the sea and no more. The Colonel's armour was heavy.

The Emperor talked about battle honours.

Crash.

Out of the mist, perhaps half a mile from the harbour, the imperial barge appeared again. Her oars beat very, very slowly as she made for the entrance.

The crest of the legion.

Crash.

The honour of the legion.

The point of crisis, of no return, had been reached. The

movement began at the Emperor's feet where three men fell together. A wave of sick nausea swept over the parade and the ranks went down together into merciful unconsciousness. The end of the quay was piled with a hundred helpless men and a band that could hear nothing over the beating of its own devoted hearts. The Emperor looked down at them compassionately.

"Self-preservation."

Mamillius and the Emperor's guard broke from the tunnel. There were perhaps two dozen of them, men fresh from a kip in the shady garden and agreeable now to a little brisk brutality. Mamillius was flourishing his sword, chanting a blood-curdling chorus from the *Seven Against Thebes* and trying to keep step to it. At the same moment the imperial barge thumped the quay. Posthumus, dirty, dishevelled and raging, scrambled ashore. The Emperor's guard broke formation, ran forward and seized him. He threw two off and leapt at Mamillius with drawn sword, roaring like a bull. Mamillius stopped in his tracks, hands and knees pressed together, chin up. He abandoned Greek for his native tongue.

"Pax—l"

Posthumus swung his sword and the Emperor closed his eyes. He heard a gong-like sound and opened them again. Posthumus was heaving under a mob of guards. Mamillius was staggering in a circle, trying unsuccessfully to push his helmet up off his eyes.

"You rotten cad, Posthumus, you absolute outsider! Now I shall have a headache."

The Emperor got down from the sea wall.

"Who is the man Posthumus brought with him in the barge?"

The Officer of the Guard saluted.

"A prisoner, Caesar. A slave, by the looks of him."

The Emperor tapped the finger of one hand in the palm of the other.

"Escort the Heir Designate through the tunnel, and the slave with him. Two of your men can lead the Lord Mamillius. This is not the moment to extract him. Ladies, the demonstration is over. You may return to the Villa."

He paused for a moment by the tormentum and looked back at the quay. The guard of honour and the band were stirring feebly like sea-creatures of the shore at the return of the tide.

"Six of your men must hold the tunnel at all costs. They must not stand aside except at your personal order."

"Caesar."

"The remainder can stand by in the garden. Keep them out of sight behind the hedges. At the double."

"Caesar."

The gardens had retained their tranquillity. The Emperor stood by the lily-pond, breathing the aromatic air gratefully. Below him the surface of the sea had begun to appear again. When his breathing was even he turned to the little group of men.

"Will you behave, Posthumus, if I tell the guard to let you go?"

Posthumus glanced at the dark mouth of the tunnel and the Emperor shook his head.

"Please put the idea of bolting through the tunnel out of your head. The men there have their orders. Come! Let us discuss things reasonably."

Posthumus shook himself free.

"What have you done to my soldiers you—sorcerer?"

"Just an inspection, Posthumus, just the usual line. But I produced it to infinity."

Posthumus reached up and settled his helmet. The scarlet and gold plume was singed.

"What are you going to do with me?"

The Emperor smiled wryly.

"Look at Mamillius. Can you imagine him as an Emperor?"

Mamillius was lying across a stone seat on his stomach. Two soldiers held his legs. At the other end a third soldier was heaving back on the jammed helmet.

"The agent's reports were circumstantial."

The Emperor crooked his finger.

"Phanocles."

"Caesar."

"Tell the Heir Designate once and for all what you were going to do."

"I told him, Caesar. No slaves, no war."

Posthumus sneered.

"Bring the slave I caught. He was one of those who burned your ship."

Two soldiers frog-marched the slave forward. He was naked, though the water had dried off him. He was a man to tear a lion apart, bearded, broad, dark and wild.

The Emperor looked him up and down.

"What is he?"

A soldier seized the man's hair, twisted his head sideways and up so that he grinned with pain. Posthumus leaned forward and inspected the notches cut in the slave's ear. He nodded and the soldier let go.

"Why did you do it?"

The slave answered him in a voice at once hoarse with shouting and clumsy with disuse.

"I am a rower."

The Emperor's eyebrows climbed.

"In future I must have rowers chained to their oars, or would that be too expensive?"

The slave tried to clasp his hands.

"Caesar—be merciful. We could not kill that man."

"Phanocles?"

"His demon protected him. A plank killed the slave by his side. The crab missed him."

Mamillius came out of his helmet with a shriek. He hurried to the Emperor.

"Mamillius—the crab was not meant for you!"

Mamillius turned excitedly to the slave.

"You did not try to kill me?"

"Why should we, lord? If you use us up, you have a right to. We were bought. But this man does not use us at all. We saw his ship move without oars or sails and against the wind. What use will there be for rowers?"

Phanocles cried out.

"My ship would have set you free!"

The Emperor looked down at the slave thoughtfully.

"Are you happy on your bench?"

"The gods know what we suffer."

"Why then?"

The slave paused for a moment. When he spoke again the words came by rote out of some deep well of the past.

" 'I had rather be slave to a smallholder than rule in hell over all the ghosts of men.' "

"I see."

The Emperor nodded to the soldiers.

"Take him away."

Posthumus laughed unpleasantly.

"That was what a professional sailor thinks of your ship, Greek!"

The Emperor raised his voice.

"Wait. Let us have the verdict of a professional soldier on the thunder-machine. Officer!"

But the officer was already saluting.

"Excuse me, Caesar, but the lady—"

"What lady?"

"They won't let her pass without my orders, Caesar."

Mamillius shouted in his broken voice.

"Euphrosyne!"

The officer came down from the salute.

"Let the lady pass, lads. Jump to it!"

The soldiers parted from the end of the tunnel and Euphrosyne came, hurrying and shrinking, to Phanocles and the Emperor.

"Where have you been, child? Why weren't you with the others? The quay is dangerous without me!"

But she still said nothing, and the veil shook against her mouth. The Emperor beckoned.

"Stand by me. You are safe now."

He turned back to the officer.

"Officer."

"Caesar."

"Stand easy. Posthumus, ask your questions."

Posthumus surveyed him for a moment.

"Captain. Do you enjoy the prospect of a battle?"

"In defence of the Father of his Country—"

The Emperor waved his hand.

"Your loyalty is not in question. Answer, please."

The Captain thought.

"On the whole, yes, Caesar."

"Why?"

"Make's a change, Caesar. Excitement, promotion, perhaps loot—and so on."

"Would you prefer to destroy your enemies at a distance?"

"I don't understand."

Posthumus jerked a thumb sideways at Phanocles.

"This slimy Greek has made that weapon on the quay. You press the tit and the enemy goes up in smoke."

The Captain ruminated.

"Has the Father of his Country no further use for his soldiers, then?"

Posthumus looked meaningly at the Captain.

"Apparently not. But I have."

"But sir—suppose the enemy gets this thunder-machine himself?"

Posthumus looked at Phanocles.

"Will armour be any use?"

"None, I should say."

The Emperor took Mamillius by the scarlet cloak and tugged it gently.

"I imagine this sort of uniform will disappear. You will spend your war crawling round on your belly. Your uniform will be mud- or dung-coloured."

The officer glanced down at his glittering breastplate.

"—and you could always paint the metal a neutral tint or just let it get dirty."

The officer paled.

"You are joking, Caesar."

"You saw what his ship did in the harbour."

The officer stepped back. His mouth was open and he was breathing quickly like a man in the first stages of nightmare. He began to glance round him, at the hedges, the stone seats, the soldiers blocking the tunnel—

Posthumus strode forward and grasped him by the arm.

"Well, Captain?"

Their eyes met. Doubt left the Captain's face. His jaw jutted and the muscles of his cheeks stood out.

"Can you manage the others, General?"

Posthumus nodded.

Instantly there was a confusion. Through a frieze of gesticulating figures, through an entanglement of men who sought to save their balance on the edge of the pond, Phanocles was visible sailing away from Posthumus' fist out over the quiet lilies. Then the officer was running fast toward the entrance of the tunnel and Posthumus was lumbering behind him. The officer shouted an order at the men guarding the entrance and they sidestepped like a human screen—one, two! one, two! one, two! Posthumus and the officer vanished into the tunnel and the guard remained to one side at attention. The soldiers began to sort themselves out by the pool. Mamillius, who had the whole width of the pool between him and the tunnel, was dashing this way and that as his astonished mind tried to find the quickest way round it. Only the Emperor still silent and distinguished, a little paler, perhaps, a little more remote as the certainty of downfall and death settled on him. Then the soldiers had picked themselves up, Phanocles had clambered out of the pool through which Mamillius, his problem solved, was now wading. Hesitating and unbelieving at the officer's defection they converged on the mouth of the tunnel. The Emperor strolled after them. He gazed thoughtfully at the human screen that discipline had rendered so ineffective. He shrugged slightly inside his toga.

He spoke very gently, as to children.

"You may stand easy."

A sudden push of air through the tunnel moved them and let them go. Almost at the same moment the ground jumped and noise hit them like the blow of a fist. The Emperor turned to Mamillius.

"Thunder?"

"Vesuvius?"

There was a whining sound from the air over the headland that separated the garden from the port, a descending whine, a brazen clang near at hand and the whisper of yew branches. The timeless moment of shock dulled for them the immediacy of their danger so that they looked at each other foolishly. Phanocles was shaking. Then there were footsteps in the tunnel, coming hastily, running, staggering. A soldier burst out of the entrance and they saw from the red and yellow favour that he was one of Posthumus' men.

"Caesar—"

"Pull yourself together. Then make your report."

"He is dead—"

"Who is dead and how did it happen?"

The soldier swayed back, then recovered.

"How can I tell you, Caesar? We were getting fell in again after the—after the inspection. General Posthumus came running from the tunnel. He saw that some of our company were away fighting the fires and he began to call out to the rest of us. There was one of your officers running behind him. I saw the officer bend down by the mark VII. There was a flash of lightning, a thunder-clap—"

"And a smoking hole in the quay. Where is Posthumus?"

The soldier spread his arms in a gesture of ignorance. Phanocles fell on his knees and put out a hand to the hem of the Emperor's toga. But the soldier was looking past them to the nearer yew hedge between the pool and the ascent of the gardens. They saw his eyes widen terribly. He screamed and took to his heels.

"Sorcery!"

Posthumus was watching them, must be watching them from behind the yew hedge, for they could see his bronze helmet with the scarlet and gold plume on it. He appeared to be cooking a small meal, for the air above his helmet shook with more than summer's heat. They saw that the plume was turning slowly to brown. The sprigs of yew bent, curled in the heat, gave way. The helmet bowed, turned among the branches and hung with its empty interior towards them.

"Come here, my man."

The soldier crept out of hiding.

"The All-Father has destroyed General Posthumus before the eyes of you and your companions for the sin of open rebellion against the Emperor. Tell them."

He turned to Phanocles.

"Go and save what you can. You are heavily in debt with humanity. Go with them, Mamillius, for you are in charge. There is an occasion waiting for you through the tunnel. Rise to it."

Their steps echoed in the tunnel and died away.

"Come, lady."

He sat down on one of the stone seats by the lily-pool.

"Stand before me."

She came, stood, but the grace of movement was gone.

"Give it me."

For a while she said nothing, but stood defended by her draperies. The Emperor said nothing but allowed the silent authority of his outstretched hand to do its work. Then she shoved the thing at him, left it in his hand and raised her own to her hidden face. The Emperor looked down at his palm thoughtfully.

"I owe my life to you it seems. Not that Posthumus wouldn't have made a better job of ruling. Lady, I must see your face."

She said nothing, did nothing. The Emperor watched her, then nodded as though they had been in explicit communion.

"I understand."

He got up, walked round the pool and stood looking over the cliff at the now visible waves.

"Let this remain another bit of history that is better forgotten."

He pitched the brass butterfly into the sea.

L'ENVOY

The Emperor and Phanocles lay opposite each other on either side of a low table. The table, the floor, the room, were circular and surrounded by pillars that held up a shadowy cupola. A constellation hung glittering in the opening directly over their heads but the room itself was lit softly from lights placed behind the pillars—warm light, congenial to leisure and digestion. A flute meditated somewhere.

"Will it work, do you think?"

"Why not, Caesar?"

"Strange man. You ponder thus and thus on universal law and evolve a certainty. Of course it will work. I must be patient."

They were silent for a while. The eunuch voice joined and commented on the flute.

"What was Mamillius doing when you left him, Phanocles?"

"He was giving many orders."

"Excellent."

"They were the wrong orders, but men were obeying him."

"That is the secret. He will be a terrible Emperor. Better than Caligula but less talented than Nero."

"He was so proud of the scar in his helmet. He said he had discovered that he was a man of action."

"So much for poetry. Poor Mamillius."

"No, Caesar. He said that action brought out the poet in him and that he had created the perfect poem in action."

"Not an epic, surely?"

"An epigram, Caesar. 'Euphrosyne is beautiful but dumb.'"

The Emperor inclined his head gravely.

"Whereas you and I know that she is exteremely clever and quick-witted."

Phanocles lifted a little on his couch.

"How could you know that?"

The Emperor rolled a grape backwards and forwards under his finger.

"I shall marry her, of course. Do not gape at me, Phanocles, or fear that I shall have you strangled when I see her face. At my age, unfortunately, it will be a marriage in name only. But it will give her security and secrecy and a measure of peace. She has a harelip, has she not?"

The blood suffused Phanocles' face, seemed to drown him and make his eyes bolt. The Emperor wagged a finger.

"Only a young fool like Mamillius could mistake her pathological shyness for a becoming modesty. I whisper this down to you from the pinnacle of a long experience and hope no woman may hear: but we men invented modesty. I wonder if we invented chastity as well? No beautiful woman could possibly refuse to show her face for so long if it were unblemished."

"I did not dare tell you."

"Because you saw that I entertained you for her sake? Alas for Mamillius and romantic love. Perseus and Andromeda! How he will dislike me. I ought to have remembered from the first that an Emperor cannot enjoy a normal human relationship."

"I am sorry—"

"So am I, Phanocles, and not wholly for myself. Did you never think to turn the light of your extraordinary intellect on Medicine?"

"No, Caesar."

"Shall I tell you why?"

"I am listening."

The Emperor's words were clear and gentle, dropping in the quiet room like tiny stones.

"I said you are hubristic. You are also selfish. You are alone in your universe with natural law and people are an interruption, an intrusion. I am selfish too and alone—but with the shape of people acknowledged to have a certain right to independent existence. Oh, you natural philosophers! Are there many of you, I wonder? Your single-minded and devoted selfishness, your royal preoccupation with the only thing that can interest you, could go near to wiping life off the earth as I wipe the bloom from this grape."

His nostrils quivered.

"But silence now. Here comes the trout."

However there was a ritual of this too, entry of the major-domo and the service, more patterns of movement. The Emperor broke his own commandment.

"Are you too young, I wonder? Or do you find as I do that when you read a book you once liked, half the pleasure is evocation of the time when you first read it? You see how selfish I am, Phanocles! If I were to read the eclogues I should not be transported to a Roman Arcady. I should be a boy again, preparing the next day's passage for my tutor."

Phanocles was recovering.

"A poor return for reading, Caesar."

"Do you think so? Surely we selfish men comprise all history in our own lives! Each of us discovers the pyramids. Space, time, life—what I might call the four-dimensional continuum—but you see how ill-adapted Latin is to philosophy! Life is a personal matter with a single fixed point of reference. Alexander did not fight his wars until I discovered him at the age of seven. When I was a baby, time was an instant; but I pushed, smelled, tasted, saw, heard, bawled that one suffocating point into whole palaces of history and vast fields of space."

"Again I do not understand you, Caesar."

"You should, for I report on an experience common to us both. But you lack my introversion—or shall I say selfishness? —see how prone an uninterrupted Emperor is to parenthesis! —and therefore you cannot distinguish it. Think, Phanocles! If you can restore to me not the gratification of an appetite, but a single precious memory! How else but by the enlargements of anticipation and memory does our human instant differ from the mindless movement of nature's clock?"

Phanocles glanced up at the constellation that hung so near and bright that they might have thought it deepened by a third dimension; but before he could think of anything to say the dishes were in place. The covers were lifted, and the sweet steam came with them. The Emperor closed his eyes, held his head forward and breathed in.

"Yes—?"

Then in accents of profound emotion:

"Yes!"

Phanocles ate his trout quickly, for he was hungry, and wished that the Emperor would give him a chance to drink too. But the Emperor was in a trance. His lips were moving and the colour came and went in his face.

"Freshness. Levels of shining water and shadows and cataracts from the dark rock on high.

"It comes back to me. I am lying on a rock that is only just as big as my body. The cliffs rise about me, the river runs by me and the water is dark for all the sun. Two pigeons discourse musically and monotonously. There is pain in my right side, for the edge of the rock cuts me: but I lie face-downward, my right arm moving slowly as a water-snail on a lump of stone. I touch a miracle of present actuality, I stroke —I am fiercely, passionately alive—a moment more and the exultation of my heart will burst in a fury of movement. But I still my ambition, my desire, my lust—I balance passion with will. I stroke slowly as a drifting weed. She lies there in the darkness, undulating, stemming the flow of water. Now—! A convulsion of two bodies, sense of terror, of rape—she flies in the air and I grab with lion's claws. She is out, she is mine—"

The Emperor opened his eyes and looked across at Phanocles. A tear trickled on his cheek exactly above the untasted fish.

"—my first trout."

He seized a cup, spilt a drop or two on the floor then held the cup up towards Phanocles.

"To the pressure cooker. The most Promethean discovery of them all."

After a while he mastered his emotion and laughed a little.

"I wonder how I am to reward you?"

"Caesar!"

Phanocles gulped and spluttered.

"My explosive—"

"I take no account of the steamship. She is amusing but expensive. I must admit that the experimentalist in me was interested in her atrocious activities, but once is enough. You must make no more steamships."

"But Caesar!"

"Besides, how can you find your way without a wind?"

"I might invent a mechanism which pointed constantly in one direction."

"By all means invent it. Perhaps you could invent a movable arrow that pointed constantly to Rome."

"Something that would point to the North."

"But no more steamships."

"I—"

The Emperor waved his hand.

"It is our Imperial will, Phanocles."

"I bow."

"She was dangerous."

"Perhaps one day, Caesar, when men are free because they no longer believe themselves to be slaves—"

The Emperor shook his head.

"You work among perfect elements and therefore politically you are an idealist. There will always be slaves though the name may change. What is slavery but the domination of the weak by the strong? How can you make them equal? Or are you fool enough to think that men are born equal?"

He was suddenly grave.

"As for your explosive—it has preserved me this day and therefore the peace of the Empire. But it has cost the Empire a merciless ruler who would have murdered half a dozen people and given justice to a hundred million. The world has lost a bargain. No, Phanocles. We will restore Jove's own bolt to his random and ineluctible hand."

"But they were my greatest inventions!"

The first trout had disappeared, cold from the Emperor's plate. Another had descended and again he immersed his face in its fragrance.

"The pressure cooker. I shall reward you for that."

"Then, Caesar, how will you reward me for this?"

"For what?"

"My third invention. I have kept it in reserve."

His hand went slowly, dramatically, to his belt. The Emperor watched him apprehensively.

"Has this any connection with thunder?"

"With silence only."

The Emperor frowned. He held a paper in either hand and glanced from one to the other.

"Poems? You are a poet then?"

"Mamillius wrote it."

"I might have known. Sophocles, Carcides—how well read the boy is!"

"This will make him famous. Read the other poem, Caesar, for it is exactly the same. I have invented a method of multiplying books. I call it printing."

"But this is—another pressure cooker!"

"A man and a boy can make a thousand copies of a book in a day."

The Emperor looked up from the two papers.

"We could give away a hundred thousand copies of Homer!"

"A million if you like."

"No poet need pine for lack of an audience—"

"Nor for money. No more dictating an edition to a handful of slaves, Caesar. A poet will sell his poems by the sack like vegetables. The very scullions will solace themselves with the glories of our Athenian drama—"

The Emperor rose to a sitting position in his enthusiasm.
"A Public Library in every town!"
"—in every home."
"Ten thousand copies of the love poems of Catullus—"
"A hundred thousand of the works of Mamillius—"
"Hesiod in every cottage—"
"An author in every street—"
"An alpine range of meticulous enquiry and information on every conceivable topic—"
"Knowledge, education—"
The Emperor lowered himself again.
"Wait. Is there enough genius to go round? How often is a Horace born?"
"Come, Caesar. Nature is bountiful."
"Supposing we all write books?"
"Why not? Interesting biographies—"
The Emperor was gazing intently at a point out of this world—somewhere in the future.
"Diary of a Provincial Governor. I Built Hadrian's Wall. My Life in Society, by a Lady of Quality."
"Scholarship, then."
"Fifty interpolated passages in the catalogue of ships. Metrical innovations in the Mimes of Herondas. The Unconscious Symbolism of the first book of Euclid. Prologomena to the Investigation of Residual Trivia."
Terror appeared in the Emperor's eyes.
"History—In the Steps of Thucydides. I was Nero's Grandmother."
Phanocles sat up and clapped his hands enthusiastically.
"Reports, Caesar, essential facts!"
The terror grew.
"—Military, Naval, Sanitary, Eugenic—I shall have to read them all! Political, Economic, Pastoral, Horticultural, Personal, Impersonal, Statistical, Medical—"
The Emperor staggered to his feet. His hands were lifted, his eyes were shut and his face was contorted.
"Let him sing again!"
Masterful and unimpassioned.
The Emperor opened his eyes. He went quickly to one of the pillars and stroked the factual stone for reassurance. He

looked up to the ceiling and gazed at the tiled constellation that hung, sparkling, in the crystal spheres. He calmed himself though his body still shivered slightly. He turned and looked across at Phanocles.

"But we were speaking of your reward."

"I am in Caesar's hands."

The Emperor came close and looked at him with quivering lips.

"Would you like to be an ambassador?"

"My highest ambition has never—"

"You would have time then to invent your instrument which points to the North. You can take your explosive and your printing with you. I shall make you Envoy Extraordinary and Plenipotentiary."

He paused for a moment.

"Phanocles, my dear friend. I want you to go to China."

The Future

———————————

CONSIDER HER WAYS

by John Wyndham

There was nothing but myself.

I hung in a timeless, spaceless, forceless void that was neither light, nor dark. I had entity, but no form; awareness, but no senses; mind, but no memory. I wondered, is this—this nothingness—my soul? And it seemed that I had wondered that always, and should go on wondering it for ever. . . .

But, somehow, timelessness ceased. I became aware that there was a force: that I was being moved, and that spacelessness had, therefore, ceased, too. There was nothing to show that I moved; I knew simply that I was being drawn. I felt happy because I knew there was something or someone to whom I wanted to be drawn. I had no other wish than to turn like a compass-needle and then fall through the void. . . .

But I was disappointed. No smooth, swift fall followed. Instead, other forces fastened on me. I was pulled this way, and then that. I did not know how I knew it; there was no outside reference, no fixed point, no direction even; yet I could feel that I was tugged hither and thither, as though against the resistance of some inner gyroscope. It was as if one force were in command of me for a time, only to weaken and lose me to a new force. Then I would seem to slide towards some unknown point, until I was arrested, and diverted upon another course. I wafted this way and that, with the sense of awareness continually growing firmer; and I wondered whether rival forces were fighting for me, good and evil, perhaps, or life and death. . . .

The sense of pulling back and forth became more definite until I was almost jerked from one course to another. Then, abruptly, the feeling of struggle finished. I had a sense of travelling faster and faster still, plunging like a wandering meteorite that had been trapped at last. . . .

"All right," said a voice. "Resuscitation was a little retarded, for some reason. Better make a note of that on her

63

card. What's the number? Oh, only her fourth time. Yes, certainly make a note. It's all right. Here she comes!"

It was a woman's voice speaking, with a slightly unfamiliar accent. The surface I was lying on shook under me. I opened my eyes, saw the ceiling moving along above me, and let them close. Presently, another voice, again with an unfamiliar intonation, spoke to me:

"Drink this," she said.

A hand lifted my head, and a cup was pressed against my lips. After I had drunk the stuff I lay back with my eyes closed again. I dozed for a little while, and came out of it feeling stronger. For some minutes I lay looking up at the ceiling and wondering vaguely where I was. I could not recall any ceiling that was painted just this pinkish shade of cream. Then, suddenly, while I was still gazing up at the ceiling, I was shocked, just as if something had hit my mind a sharp blow. I was frighteningly aware that it was not just the pinkish ceiling that was unfamiliar—everything was unfamiliar. Where there should have been memories there was just a great gap. I had no idea who I was, or where I was; I could recall nothing of how or why I came to be here. . . . In a rush of panic I tried to sit up, but a hand pressed me back, and presently held the cup to my lips again.

"You're quite all right. Just relax," the same voice told me, reassuringly.

I wanted to ask questions, but somehow I felt immensely weary, and everything was too much trouble. The first rush of panic subsided, leaving me lethargic. I wondered what had happened to me—had I been in an accident, perhaps? Was this the kind of thing that happened when one was badly shocked? I did not know, and now for the moment I did not care: I was being looked after. I felt so drowsy that the questions could wait.

I suppose I dozed, and it may have been for a few minutes, or for an hour. I know only that when I opened my eyes again I felt calmer—more puzzled than alarmed—and I lay for a time without moving. I had recovered enough grasp now to console myself with the thought that if there had been an accident, at least there was no pain.

Presently I gained a little more energy, and, with it, curiosity to know where I was. I rolled my head on the pillow to see more of the surroundings.

A few feet away I saw a contrivance on wheels, something between a bed and a trolley. On it, asleep with her mouth open, was the most enormous woman I had ever seen. I stared, wondering whether it was some kind of cage over her to take the weight of the covers that gave her the mountainous look, but the movement of her breathing soon showed me that it was not. Then I looked beyond her and saw two more trolleys, both supporting equally enormous women.

I studied the nearest one more closely, and discovered to my surprise that she was quite young—not more than twenty-two, or twenty-three, I guessed. Her face was a little plump, perhaps, but by no means over-fat; indeed, with her fresh, healthy young colouring and her short-cropped gold curls, she was quite pretty. I fell to wondering what curious disorder of the glands could cause such a degree of anomaly at her age.

Ten minutes or so passed, and there was a sound of brisk, business-like footsteps approaching. A voice inquired:

"How are you feeling now?"

I rolled my head to the other side, and found myself looking into a face almost level with my own. For a moment I thought its owner must be a child, then I saw that the features under the white cap were certainly not less than thirty years old. Without waiting for a reply she reached under the bed-clothes and took my pulse. Its rate appeared to satisfy her, for she nodded confidently.

"You'll be all right now, Mother," she told me.

I stared at her, blankly.

"The car's only just outside the door there. Do you think you can walk it?" she went on.

Bemusedly, I asked:

"What car?"

"Why, to take you home, of course," she said, with professional patience. "Come along now." And she pulled away the bedclothes.

I started to move, and looked down. What I saw there held me fixed. I lifted my arm. It was like nothing so much as a plump, white bolster with a ridiculous little hand attached at the end. I stared at it in horror. Then I heard a far-off scream as I fainted. . . .

When I opened my eyes again there was a woman—a normal-sized woman—in a white overall with a stethoscope round her neck, frowning at me in perplexity. The white-capped woman I had taken for a child stood beside her, reaching only a little above her elbow.

"—I don't know, Doctor," she was saying. "She just suddenly screamed and fainted."

"What is it? What's happened to me? I know I'm not like this—I'm not, I'm not," I said, and I could hear my own voice wailing the words.

The doctor went on looking puzzled.

"What does she mean?" she asked.

"I've no idea, Doctor," said the small one. "It was quite sudden, as if she'd had some kind of shock—but I don't know why."

"Well, she's been passed and signed-off, and, anyway, she can't stay here. We need the room," said the doctor. "I'd better give her a sedative."

"But what's happened? Who am I? There's something terribly wrong. I know I'm not like this. P-please t-tell me—" I implored her, and then somehow lost myself in a stammer and a muddle.

The doctor's manner became soothing. She laid a hand gently on my shoulder.

"That's all right, Mother. There's nothing to worry about. Just take things quietly. We'll soon have you back home."

Another white-capped assistant, no taller than the first, hurried up with a syringe, and handed it to the doctor.

"No!" I protested. "I want to know where I am. Who am I? Who are you? What's happened to me?" I tried to slap the syringe out of her hand, but both the small assistants flung themselves on my arm, and held on to it while she pressed in the needle.

It was a sedative, all right. It did not put me out, but it detached me. An odd feeling: I seemed to be floating a few feet outside myself and considering me with an unnatural calmness. I was able, or felt that I was able, to evaluate matters with intelligent clarity. Evidently I was suffering from amnesia.

A shock of some kind had caused me to 'lose my memory', as it is often put. Obviously it was only a very small part of my memory that had gone—just the personal part—who I was, what I was, where I lived—all the mechanism for day-to-day getting along seemed to be intact: I'd not forgotten how to talk, or how to think, and I seemed to have quite a well-stored mind to think with.

On the other hand there was a nagging conviction that everything about me was somehow wrong. I knew, somehow, that I'd never before seen the place I was in; I knew, too, that there was something queer about the presence of the two small nurses; above all, I knew, with absolute certainty, that this massive form lying here was not mine. I could not recall what face I ought to see in a mirror, not even whether it would be dark or fair, or old or young, but there was no shadow of doubt in my mind that, whatever it was like, it had never topped such a shape as I had now.

—And there were the other enormous young women, too. Obviously, it could not be a matter of glandular disorder in all of us, or there'd not be this talk of sending me 'home', wherever that might be. . . .

I was still arguing the situation with myself in, thanks no doubt to the sedative, a most reasonable-seeming manner, though without making any progress at all, when the ceiling above my head began to move again, and I realized I was being wheeled along. Doors opened at the end of the room, and the trolley tilted a little beneath me as we went down a gentle ramp beyond.

At the foot of the ramp, an ambulance-like car, with pink coachwork polished until it gleamed, was waiting with the rear doors open. I observed interestedly that I was playing a part in a routine procedure. A team of eight diminutive attendants carried out the task of transferring me from the trolley to a sprung couch in the ambulance as if it were a kind of drill. Two of them lingered after the rest to tuck in my coverings and place another pillow behind my head. Then they got out, closing the doors behind them, and in a minute or two we started off.

It was at this point—and possibly the sedative helped in this, too—that I began to have an increasing sense of balance and a feeling that I was perceiving the situation. Probably there had been an accident, as I had suspected, but obviously my error, and the chief cause of my alarm, proceeded from my assumption that I was a stage further on than I actually was. I had assumed that after an interval I had recovered consciousness in these baffling circumstances, whereas the true state of affairs must clearly be that I had not recovered consciousness. I must be still in a suspended state, very likely with concussion, and this was a dream, or hallucination. Presently, I should wake up in conditions that would at least be sensible, if not necessarily familiar.

I wondered now that this consoling and stabilizing thought had not occurred to me before, and decided that it was the alarming sense of detailed reality that had thrown me into panic. It had been astonishingly stupid of me to be taken in to the extent of imagining that I really was a kind of Gulliver among rather over-size Lilliputians. It was quite characteristic of most dreams, too, that I should lack a clear knowledge of my identity, so we did not need to be surprised at that. The thing to do was to take an intelligent interest in all I observed: the whole thing must be chockful of symbolic content which it would be most interesting to work out later.

The discovery quite altered my attitude and I looked about me with a new attention. It struck me as odd right away that here was so much circumstantial detail, and all of it in focus—there was none of that sense of foreground in sharp relief against a muzzy, or even non-existent, background that one usually meets in a dream. Everything was presented with a most convincing, three-dimensional solidity. My own sensations, too, seemed perfectly valid. The injection, in particular, had been quite acutely authentic. The illusion of reality fascinated me into taking mental notes with some care.

The interior of the van, or ambulance, or whatever it was, was finished in the same shell-pink as the outside—except for the roof, which was powder-blue with a scatter of small silver stars. Against the front partition were mounted several cupboards, with plated handles. My couch, or stretcher, lay along the left side: on the other were two fixed seats, rather small, and upholstered in a semi-glazed material to match the colour of the rest. Two long windows on each side left little solid wall. Each of them was provided with curtains of a fine net, gathered back now in pink braid loops, and had a roller blind furled above it. Simply by turning my head on the pillow I was able to observe the passing scenery—though somewhat jerkily, for either the springing of the vehicle scarcely matched its appointments, or the road surface was bad: whichever the cause, I was glad my own couch was independently and quite comfortably sprung.

The external view did not offer a great deal of variety save in its hues. Our way was lined by buildings standing back behind some twenty yards of tidy lawn. Each block was three storeys high, about fifty yards long, and had a tiled roof of somewhat low pitch, suggesting a vaguely Italian influence. Structurally the blocks appeared identical, but each was differently coloured, with contrasting window-frames and doors, and carefully considered, uniform curtains. I could see no one behind the windows; indeed there appeared to be no one about at all except here and there a woman in overalls mowing a lawn, or tending one of the inset flowerbeds.

Further back from the road, perhaps two hundred yards away, stood larger, taller, more utilitarian-looking blocks, some of them with high, factory-type chimneys. I thought they might actually be factories of some kind, but at the distance, and because I had no more than fugitive views of them between the foreground blocks, I could not be sure.

The road itself seldom ran straight for more than a hundred yards at a stretch, and its windings made one wonder whether the buildings had not been more concerned to follow a contour line than a direction. There was little other traffic, and what there was consisted of lorries, large or small, mostly large. They were painted in one primary colour or other, with only a five-fold combination of letters and figures on their sides for further identification. In design they might have been any lorries anywhere.

We continued this uneventful progress at a modest pace for some twenty minutes, until we came to a stretch where the road was under repair. The car slowed, and the workers moved to one side, out of our way. As we crawled forward over the broken surface I was able to get a good look at them. They were all women or girls dressed in denim-like trousers, sleeveless singlets and working boots. All had their hair cut quite short, and a few wore hats. They were tall and broad-shouldered, bronzed and healthy-looking. The biceps of their arms were like a man's, and the hafts of their picks and shovels rested in the hard, strong hands of manual toilers.

They watched with concern as the car edged its way on to the rough patch, but when it drew level with them they transferred their attention, and jostled and craned to look inside at me.

They smiled widely, showing strong white teeth in their browned faces. All of them raised their right hands, making some sign to me, still smiling. Their goodwill was so evident that I smiled back. They walked along, keeping pace with the crawling car, looking at me expectantly while their smiles faded into puzzlement. They were saying something but I could not hear the words. Some of them insistently repeated the sign. Their disappointed look made it clear that I was expected to respond with more than a smile. The only way that occurred to me was to raise my own right hand in imitation of their gesture. It was at least a qualified success; their faces brightened though a rather puzzled look remained. Then the car lurched on to the made-up road again and their still somewhat troubled faces slid back as we speeded up to our former sedate pace. More dream symbols, of course—but certainly not one of the stock symbols from the book. What on earth, I wondered, could a party of friendly Amazons, equipped with navvying implements instead of bows, stand for in my subconscious? Something frustrated, I imagined. A suppressed desire to dominate? I did not seem to be getting much further along that line when we passed the last of the variegated but nevertheless monotonous blocks, and ran into open country.

The flower-beds had shown me already that it was spring, and now I was able to look on healthy pastures, and neat arable fields already touched with green; there was a haze-like green smoke along the trim hedges, and some of the trees in the tidily placed spinneys were in young leaf. The sun was shining with a bright benignity upon the most precise countryside I had ever seen; only the cattle dotted about the fields introduced a slight disorder into the careful dispositions.

The farmhouses themselves were part of the pattern; hollow squares of neat buildings with an acre or so of vegetable garden on one side, an orchard on another, and a rickyard on a third. There was a suggestion of a doll's landscape about it— Grandma Moses, but tidied up and rationalized. I could see no random cottages, casually sited sheds, or unplanned outgrowths from the farm buildings. And what, I asked myself, should we conclude from this rather pathological exhibition of tidiness? That I was a more uncertain person than I had supposed, one who was subconsciously yearning for simplicity and security? Well, well. . . .

An open lorry which must have been travelling ahead of us turned off down a lane bordered by beautifully laid hedges, towards one of the farms. There were half a dozen young women in it, holding implements of some kind; Amazons, again. One of them, looking back, drew the attention of the rest to us. They raised their hands in the same sign that the others had made, and then waved cheerfully. I waved back.

Rather bewildering, I thought: Amazons for domination and this landscape for passive security: the two did not seem to tie up very well.

We trundled on, at our unambitious pace of twenty miles an hour or so, for what I guessed to be three-quarters of an hour, with the prospect changing very little. The country undulated gently and appeared to continue like that to the foot of a line of low, blue hills many miles away. The tidy farmhouses went by with almost the regularity of milestones, though with something like twice the frequency. Occasionally there were working-parties in the fields; more rarely, one saw individuals busy about the farms, and others hoeing with tractors, but they were all too far off for me to make out any details. Presently, however, came a change.

Off to the left of the road, stretching back at right-angles to it for more than a mile, appeared a row of trees. At first I thought it just a wood, but then I noticed that the trunks were evenly spaced, and the trees themselves topped and pruned until they gave more the impression of a high fence.

The end of it came to within twenty feet of the road, where it turned, and we ran along beside it for almost half a mile until the car slowed, turned to the left and stopped in front of a pair of tall gates. There were a couple of toots on the horn.

The gates were ornamental, and possibly of wrought iron under their pink paint. The archway that they barred was stucco-covered, and painted the same colour.

Why, I inquired of myself, this prevalence of pink, which I regard as a namby-pamby colour, anyway? Flesh-colour? Symbolic of an ardency for the flesh which I had insufficiently gratified? I scarcely thought so. Not pink. Surely a burning red. . . . I don't think I know anyone who can be really ardent in a pink way. . . .

While we waited, a feeling that there was something wrong with the gatehouse grew upon me. The structure was a single-storey building, standing against the left, inner side of the archway, and coloured to match it. The woodwork was pale blue, and there were white net curtains at the windows. The door opened, and a middle-aged woman in a white blouse-and-trouser suit came out. She was bare-headed, with a few grey locks in her short, dark hair. Seeing me, she raised her hand in the same sign the Amazons had used, though perfunctorily, and walked over to open the gates. It was only as she pushed them back to admit us that I suddenly saw how small she was —certainly not over four feet tall. And that explained what was wrong with the gatehouse: it was built entirely to her scale. . . .

I went on staring at her and her little house as we passed. Well, what about that? Mythology is rich in gnomes and 'little people', and they are fairly pervasive of dreams, too. Somebody, I was sure, must have decided that they are a standard symbol of something, but for the moment I did not recall what it was. Would it be repressed philo-progenitive-ness, or was that too unsubtle? I stowed that away, too, for later contemplation and brought my attention back to the surroundings.

We were on our way, unhurriedly, along something more like a drive than a road, with surroundings that suggested a compromise between a public garden and a municipal housing estate. There were wide lawns of an unblemished velvet green, set here and there with flower-beds, delicate groups of silver birch, and occasional larger, single trees. Among them stood pink, three-storey blocks, dotted about, seemingly to no particular plan.

A couple of the Amazon-types in singlets and trousers of a faded rust-red were engaged in planting-out a bed close beside the drive, and we had to pause while they dragged their hand-cart full of tulips on to the grass to let us pass. They gave me the usual salute and amiable grin as we went by.

A moment later I had a feeling that something had gone wrong with my sight, but as we passed one block we came in sight of another. It was white instead of pink, but otherwise exactly similar to the rest—except that it was scaled down by at least one-third. . . .

I blinked at it and stared hard, but it continued to seem just the same size.

A little further on, a grotesquely huge woman in pink draperies was walking slowly and heavily across a lawn. She was accompanied by three of the small, white-suited women looking, in contrast, like children, or very animated dolls: one was involuntarily reminded of tugs fussing round a liner.

I began to feel swamped: the proliferation and combination of symbols was getting well out of my class.

The car forked to the right, and presently we drew up before a flight of steps leading to one of the pink buildings— a normal-sized building, but still not free from oddity, for the steps were divided by a central balustrade; those to the left of it were normal, those to right, smaller and more numerous.

Three toots on the horn announced our arrival. In about ten seconds half a dozen small women appeared in the door-way and came running down the right-hand side of the steps. A door slammed as the driver got out and went to meet them. When she came into my range of view I saw that she was one of the little ones, too, but not in white as the rest were; she wore a shining pink suit like a livery that exactly matched the car.

They had a word together before they came round to open the door behind me, then a voice said brightly:

"Welcome, Mother Orchis. Welcome home."

The couch or stretcher slid back on runners, and between them they lowered it to the ground. One young woman whose

blouse was badged with a pink St. Andrew's cross on the
left breast leaned over me. She inquired considerately:

"Do you think you can walk, Mother?"

It did not seem the moment to inquire into the form of
address. I was obviously the only possible target for the
question.

"Walk?" I repeated. "Of course I can walk." And I sat up,
with about eight hands assisting me.

'Of course' had been an overstatement. I realized that by
the time I had been heaved to my feet. Even with all the
help that was going on around me it was an exertion which
brought on heavy breathing. I looked down at the monstrous
form that billowed under my pink draperies, with a sick
revulsion and a feeling that, whatever this particular mass of
symbolism disguised, it was likely to prove a distasteful revela-
tion later on. I tried a step. 'Walk' was scarcely the word for
my progress. It felt like, and must have looked like, a slow
series of forward surges. The women, at little more than
my elbow height, fluttered about me like a flock of anxious
hens. Once started, I was determined to go on, and I
progressed with a kind of wave-motion, first across a few yards
of gravel, and then, with ponderous deliberation, up the left-
hand side of the steps.

There was a perceptible sense of relief and triumph all
round as I reached the summit. We paused there a few
moments for me to regain my breath, then we moved on into
the building. A corridor led straight ahead, with three or four
closed doors on each side; at the end it branched right and
left. We took the left arm, and, at the end of it, I came face
to face, for the first time since the hallucination had set in,
with a mirror.

It took every volt of my resolution not to panic again at
what I saw in it. The first few seconds of my stare were spent
in fighting down a leaping hysteria.

In front of me stood an outrageous travesty, an elephantine
female form, looking the more huge for its pink swathings.
Mercifully, they covered everything but the head and hands,
but these exposures were themselves another kind of shock, for
the hands, though soft and dimpled and looking utterly out

of proportion, were not uncomely, and the head and face were those of a girl.

She was pretty, too. She could not have been more than twenty-one, if that. Her curling fair hair was touched with auburn lights, and cut in a kind of bob. The complexion of her face was pink and cream, her mouth was gentle, and red without any artifice. She looked back at me, and at the little women anxiously clustering round me, from a pair of blue-green eyes beneath lightly arched brows. And this delicate face, this little Fragonard, was set upon that monstrous body: no less outrageously might a blossom of freesia sprout from a turnip.

When I moved my lips, hers moved; when I bent my arm, hers bent; and yet, once I got the better of that threatening panic, she ceased to be a reflection. She was nothing like me, so she must be a stranger whom I was observing, though in a most bewildering way. My panic and revulsion gave way to sadness, an aching pity for her. I could weep for the shame of it. I did. I watched the tears brim on her lower lids; mistily, I saw them overflow.

One of the little women beside me caught hold of my hand. "Mother Orchis, dear, what's the matter?" she asked, full of concern.

I could not tell her: I had no clear idea myself. The image in the mirror shook her head, with tears running down her cheeks. Small hands patted me here and there; small, soothing voices encouraged me onward. The next door was opened for me and, amid concerned fussing, I was led into the room beyond.

We entered a place that struck me as a cross between a boudoir and a ward. The boudoir impression was sustained by a great deal of pink—in the carpet, coverlets, cushions, lampshades, and filmy window curtains; the ward motif, by an array of six divans, or couches, one of which was un-occupied.

It was a large enough room for three couches, separated by a chest, a chair and table for each, to be arranged on each side without an effect of crowding, and the open space in the middle was still big enough to contain several expansive easy chairs and a central table bearing an intricate flower-arrangement. A not displeasing scent faintly pervaded the place, and from somewhere came the subdued sound of a string quartette in a sentimental mood. Five of the bed-couches were already mountainously occupied. Two of my attendant party detached themselves and hurried ahead to turn back the pink satin cover on the sixth.

Faces from all the five other beds were turned towards me. Three of them smiling in welcome, the other two less committal.

"Hallo, Orchis," one of them greeted me in a friendly tone. Then, with a touch of concern, she added: "What's the matter, dear? Did you have a bad time?"

I looked at her. She had a kindly, plumply pretty face, framed by light brown hair as she lay back against a cushion. The face looked about twenty-three or twenty-four years old. The rest of her was a huge mound of pink satin. I couldn't make any reply, but I did my best to return her smile as we passed.

Our convoy hove-to by the empty bed. After some preparation and positioning I was helped into it by all hands, and a cushion was arranged behind my head.

The exertion of my journey from the car had been considerable, and I was thankful to relax. While two of the little women pulled up the coverlet and arranged it over me, another produced a handkerchief and dabbed gently at my cheeks. She encouraged me:

"There you are, dear. Safely home again now. You'll be quite all right when you've rested a bit. Just try to sleep for a little."

"What's the matter with her?" inquired a forthright voice from one of the other beds. "Did she make a mess of it?"

The little woman with the handkerchief—she was the one who wore the St. Andrew's cross and appeared to be in charge of the operation—turned her head sharply.

"There's no need for that tone, Mother Hazel. Of course Mother Orchis had four beautiful babies—didn't you, dear?" she added to me. "She's just a bit tired after the journey, that's all."

"H'mph," said the girl addressed, in an unaccommodating tone, but she made no further comment.

A degree of fussing continued. Presently the small woman handed me a glass of something that looked like water, but had unsuspected strength. I spluttered a little at the first taste, but quickly felt the better for it. After a little more tidying and ordering my retinue departed, leaving me propped against my cushion, with the eyes of the five other monstrous women dwelling upon me speculatively.

An awkward silence was broken by the girl who had greeted me as I came in.

"Where did they send you for your holiday, Orchis?"

"Holiday?" I asked blankly.

She and the rest stared at me in astonishment.

"I don't know what you're talking about," I told them.

They went on staring, stupidly, stolidly.

"It can't have been much of a holiday," observed one, obviously puzzled. "I'll not forget my last one. They sent me to the sea, and gave me a little car so that I could get about everywhere. Everybody was lovely to us, and there were only six Mothers there, including me. Did you go by the sea, or in the mountains?"

They were determined to be inquisitive, and one would have to make some answer sooner or later. I chose what seemed the simplest way out for the moment.

"I can't remember," I said. "I can't remember a thing. I seem to have lost my memory altogether."

That was not very sympathetically received, either.

"Oh," said the one who had been addressed as Hazel, with a degree of satisfaction. "I thought there was something. And I suppose you can't even remember for certain whether your babies were Grade One this time, Orchis?"

"Don't be stupid, Hazel," one of the others told her. "Of course they were Grade One. If they'd not been, Orchis wouldn't be back here now—she'd have been re-rated as a Class Two Mother, and sent to Whitewich." In a more kindly tone she asked me: "When did it happen, Orchis?"

"I—I don't know," I said. "I can't remember anything before this morning at the hospital. It's all gone entirely."

"Hospital!" repeated Hazel, scornfully.

"She must mean the Centre," said the other. "But do you mean to say you can't even remember us, Orchis?"

"No," I admitted, shaking my head. "I'm sorry, but everything before I came round in the Hosp—in the Centre, is all blank."

"That's queer," Hazel said, in an unsympathetic tone. "Do they know?"

One of the others took my part.

"Of course they're bound to know. I expect they don't think that remembering or not has anything to do with having Grade One babies. And why should it, anyway? But look, Orchis—"

"Why not let her rest for a bit," another cut in. "I don't suppose she's feeling too good after the Centre, and the journey, and getting in here. I never do myself. Don't take any notice of them, Orchis, dear. You just go to sleep for a bit. You'll probably find it's all quite all right when you wake up."

I accepted her suggestion gratefully. The whole thing was far too bewildering to cope with at the moment; moreover, I did feel exhausted. I thanked her for her advice, and lay back on my pillow. In so far as the closing of one's eyes can be made ostentatious, I made it so. What was more surprising was that, if one can be said to sleep within an hallucination or a dream, I slept. . . .

In the moment of waking, before opening my eyes, I had a flash of hope that I should find the illusion had spent itself. Unfortunately, it had not. A hand was shaking my shoulder gently, and the first thing that I saw was the face of the little women's leader, close to mine.

In the way of nurses she said:

"There, Mother Orchis, dear. You'll be feeling a lot better after that nice sleep, won't you?"

Beyond her, two more of the small women were carrying a short-legged bed-tray towards me. They set it down so that it bridged me and was convenient to reach. I stared at the load on it. It was, with no exception, the most enormous and nourishing meal I had ever seen put before one person. The first sight of it revolted me—but then I became aware of a schism within, for it did not revolt the physical form that I occupied: that, in fact, had a watering mouth, and was eager to begin. An inner part of me marvelled in a kind of semi-detachment while the rest consumed two or three fish, a whole chicken, some slices of meat, a pile of vegetables, fruit hidden under mounds of stiff cream, and more than a quart of milk, without any sense of surfeit. Occasional glances showed me that the other 'Mothers' were dealing just as thoroughly with the contents of their similar trays.

I caught one or two curious looks from them, but they were too seriously occupied to take up their inquisition again at the moment. I wondered how to fend them off later, and it occurred to me that if only I had a book or a magazine I might be able to bury myself effectively, if not very politely, in it.

When the attendants returned, I asked the badged one if she could let me have something to read. The effect of such a simple request was astonishing: the two who were removing my tray all but dropped it. The one beside me gaped for an amazed moment before she collected her wits. She looked at me, first with suspicion and then with concern.

"Not feeling quite yourself yet, dear?" she suggested.

"But I am," I protested. "I'm quite all right now."

The look of concern persisted, however.

"If I were you I'd try to sleep again," she advised.

"But I don't want to. I'd just like to read quietly," I objected.

She patted my shoulder, a little uncertainly.

"I'm afraid you've had an exhausting time, Mother. Never mind, I'm sure it'll pass quite soon."

I felt impatient. "What's wrong with wanting to read?" I demanded.

She smiled a smug, professional-nurse smile.

"There, there, dear. Just you try to rest a little more. Why, bless me, what on earth would a Mother want with knowing how to read?"

With that she tidied my coverlet, and bustled away, leaving me to the wide-eyed stares of my five companions. Hazel gave a kind of contemptuous snigger; otherwise there was no audible comment for several minutes.

I had reached a stage where the persistence of the hallucination was beginning to wear away my detachment. I could feel that under a little more pressure I should be losing my confidence and starting to doubt its unreality. I did not at all care for its calm continuity: inconsequent exaggerations and jumps, foolish perspectives, indeed, any of the usual dream characteristics would have been reassuring; but, instead, it continued to present obvious nonsense, with an alarming air of conviction and consequence. Effects, for instance, were unmistakably following causes. I began to have an uncomfortable feeling that were one to dig deep enough one might begin to find logical causes for the absurdities, too. The integration was far too good for mental comfort—even the fact that I had enjoyed my meal as if I were fully awake, and was consciously feeling the better for it, encouraged the disturbing quality of reality.

"Read!" Hazel said suddenly, with a scornful laugh. "And write, too, I suppose?"

"Well, why not?" I retorted.

They all gazed at me more attentively than ever, and then exchanged meaning glances among themselves. Two of them smiled at one another. I demanded irritably: "What on earth's wrong with that? Am I supposed not to be able to read or write, or something?"

One said kindly, soothingly:

"Orchis, dear. Don't you think it would be better if you were to ask to see the doctor? Just for a check-up?"

"No," I told her flatly. "There's nothing wrong with me. I'm just trying to understand. I simply ask for a book, and you all look at me as if I were mad. Why?"

After an awkward pause the same one said humouringly, and almost in the words of the little attendant:

"Orchis, dear, do try to pull yourself together. What sort of good would reading and writing be to a Mother? How could they help her to have better babies?"

"There are other things in life besides having babies," I said, shortly.

If they had been surprised before, they were thunderstruck now. Even Hazel seemed bereft of suitable comment. Their idiotic astonishment exasperated me and made me suddenly sick of the whole nonsensical business. Temporarily, I *did* forget to be the detached observer of a dream.

"Damn it," I broke out. "What *is* all this rubbish? Orchis! Mother Orchis!—for God's sake! Where am I? Is this some kind of lunatic asylum?"

I stared at them, angrily, loathing the sight of them, wondering if they were all in some spiteful complicity against me. Somehow I was quite convinced in my own mind that whoever, or whatever, I was, I was not a mother. I said so, forcibly, and then, to my annoyance, burst into tears.

For lack of anything else to use, I dabbed at my eyes with my sleeve. When I could see clearly again I found that four of them were looking at me with kindly concern. Hazel, however, was not.

"I said there was something queer about her," she told the others, triumphantly. "She's mad, that's what it is."

The one who had been most kindly disposed before, tried again:

"But, Orchis, of course you are a Mother. You're a Class One Mother—with three births registered. Twelve fine Grade One babies, dear. You *can't* have forgotten that!"

For some reason I wept again. I had a feeling that something was trying to break through the blankness in my mind; but I did not know what it was, only that it made me feel intensely miserable.

"Oh, this is cruel, cruel! Why can't I stop it? Why won't it go away and leave me?" I pleaded. "There's a horrible cruel mockery here—but I don't understand it. What's wrong with me? I'm not obsessional—I'm not—I—oh, can't somebody help me . . . ?"

I kept my eyes tight shut for a time, willing with all my mind that the whole hallucination should fade and disappear.

But it did not. When I looked again they were still there, their silly, pretty faces gaping stupidly at me across the revolting mounds of pink satin.

"I'm going to get out of this," I said.

It was a tremendous effort to raise myself to a sitting position. I was aware of the rest watching me, wide-eyed, while I made it. I struggled to get my feet round and over the side of the bed, but they were all tangled in the satin coverlet and I could not reach to free them. It was the true, desperate frustration of a dream. I heard my voice pleading: "Help me! Oh, Donald, darling, please help me. . . ."

And suddenly, as if the word 'Donald' had released a spring, something seemed to click in my head. The shutter in my mind opened, not entirely, but enough to let me know who I was. I understood, suddenly, where the cruelty had lain.

I looked at the others again. They were still staring half-bewildered, half-alarmed. I gave up the attempt to move, and lay back on my pillows again.

"You can't fool me any more," I told them. "I know who I am, now."

"But, Mother Orchis—" one began.

"Stop that," I snapped at her. I seemed to have swung suddenly out of self-pity into a kind of masochistic callousness. "I am not a mother," I said harshly. "I am just a woman who, for a short time, had a husband, and who hoped—but only hoped—that she would have babies by him."

A pause followed that; a rather odd pause, where there should have been at least a murmur. What I had said did not seem to have registered. The faces showed no understanding; they were as uncomprehending as dolls'.

Presently, the most friendly one seemed to feel an obligation to break up the silence. With a little vertical crease between her brows: "What," she inquired tentatively, "what is a husband?"

I looked hard from one face to another. There was no trace of guile in any of them; nothing but puzzled speculation such as one sometimes sees in a child's eyes. I felt close to hysteria for a moment; then I took a grip on myself. Very well, then, since the hallucination would not leave me alone, I would play it at its own game, and see what came of that. I began to explain with a kind of dead-pan, simple-word seriousness:

"A husband is a man whom a woman takes . . ."

Evidently, from their expressions I was not very enlightening. However, they let me go on for three or four sentences without interruption. Then, when I paused for breath, the kindly one chipped in with a point which she evidently felt needed clearing up:

"But what," she asked, in evident perplexity, "what is a man?"

A cool silence hung over the room after my exposition. I had an impression I had been sent to Coventry, or semi-Coventry, by them, but I did not bother to test it. I was too much occupied trying to force the door of my memory further open, and finding that beyond a certain point it would not budge.

I knew now that I was Jane. I had been Jane Summers, and had become Jane Waterleigh when I had married Donald.

I was—had been—twenty-four when we were married: just twenty-five when Donald was killed, six months later. And there it stopped. It seemed like yesterday, but I couldn't tell. . . .

Before that, everything was perfectly clear. My parents and friends, my home, my schools, my training, my job, as Dr. Summers, at the Wraychester Hospital. I could remember my first sight of Donald when they brought him in one evening with a broken leg—and all that followed. . . .

I could remember now the face that I ought to see in a looking-glass—and it was certainly nothing like that I had seen in the corridor outside—it should be more oval, with a complexion looking faintly sun-tanned; with a smaller, neater mouth; surrounded by chestnut hair that curled naturally; with brown eyes rather wide apart and perhaps a little grave as a rule.

I knew, too, how the rest of me should look—slender, long-legged, with small, firm breasts—a nice body but one that I had simply taken for granted until Donald gave me pride in it by loving it. . . .

I looked down at the repulsive mound of pink satin, and shuddered. A sense of outrage came welling up. I longed for Donald to comfort and pet me and love me and tell me it would be all right; that I wasn't as I was seeing myself at all, and that it *really* was a dream. At the same time I was stricken with horror at the thought that he should ever see me gross and obese like this. And then I remembered that Donald would never see me again at all—never any more—

and I was wretched and miserable, and the tears trickled down my cheeks again.

The five others just went on looking at me, wide-eyed and wondering. Half an hour passed, still in silence, then the door opened to admit a whole troop of the little women, all in white suits. I saw Hazel look at me, and then at the leader. She seemed about to speak, and then to change her mind. The little women split up, two to a couch. Standing one on each side, they stripped away the coverlet, rolled up their sleeves, and set to work at massage.

At first it was not unpleasant, and quite soothing. One lay back and relaxed. Presently, however, I liked it less: soon I found it offensive.

"Stop that!" I told the one on the right, sharply.

She paused, smiled at me amiably, though a trifle uncertainly, and then continued.

"I said stop it," I told her, pushing her away.

Her eyes met mine. They were troubled and hurt, although a professional smile still curved her mouth.

"I mean it," I added, curtly.

She continued to hesitate, and glanced across at her partner on the further side of the bed.

"You, too," I told the other. "That'll do."

She did not even pause in her rhythm. The one on the right plucked a decision and returned. She restarted just what I had stopped. I reached out and pushed her, harder this time. There must have been a lot more muscle in that bolster of an arm than one would have supposed. The shove carried her half across the room, and she tripped and fell.

All movement in the room suddenly ceased. Everybody stared, first at her, and then at me. The pause was brief. They all set to work again. I pushed away the girl on the left, too, though more gently. The other one picked herself up. She was crying and she looked frightened, but she set her jaw doggedly and started to come back.

"You keep away from me, you little horrors," I told them threateningly.

That checked them. They stood off, and looked miserably at one another. The one with the badge of seniority fussed up.

"What's the trouble, Mother Orchis?" she inquired.

I told her. She looked puzzled.

"But that's quite right," she expostulated.

"Not for me. I don't like it, and I won't have it," I replied. She stood awkwardly, at a loss.

Hazel's voice came from the other side of the room:

"Orchis is off her head. She's been telling us the most disgusting things. She's quite mad."

The little woman turned to regard her, and then looked inquiringly at one of the others. When the girl confirmed with a nod and an expression of distaste she turned back to me, giving me a searching inspection.

"You two go and report," she told my dicomfited masseuses.

They were both crying now, and they went wretchedly down the room together. The one in charge gave me another long, thoughtful look, and then followed them.

A few minutes later all the rest had packed-up and gone. The six of us were alone again. It was Hazel who broke the ensuing silence.

"That was a bitchy piece of work. The poor little devils were only doing their job," she observed.

"If that's their job, I don't like it," I told her.

"So you just get them a beating, poor things. But I suppose that's the lost memory again. You wouldn't remember that a Servitor who upsets a Mother is beaten, would you?" she added sarcastically.

"Beaten?" I repeated, uneasily.

"Yes, beaten," she mimicked. "But you don't care what becomes of them, do you? I don't know what's happened to you while you were away, but whatever it was it seems to have produced a thoroughly nasty result. I never did care for you, Orchis, though the others thought I was wrong. Well, now we all know."

None of the rest offered any comment. The feeling that they shared her opinion was strong, but luckily I was spared confirmation by the opening of the door.

The senior attendant re-entered with half a dozen small myrmidons, but this time the group was dominated by a handsome woman of about thirty. Her appearance gave me immense relief. She was neither little, nor Amazonian, nor was she huge. Her present company made her look a little over-tall, perhaps, but I judged her at about five foot ten; a normal, pleasant-featured young woman with brown hair, cut somewhat short, and a pleated black skirt showing beneath a white overall. The senior attendant was almost trotting to keep up with her longer steps, and was saying something about delusions and 'only from the Centre to-day, Doctor.'

The woman stopped beside my couch while the smaller women huddled together, looking at me with some misgiving. She thrust a thermometer into my mouth and held my wrist. Satisfied on both these counts, she inquired:

"Headache? Any other aches or pains?"

"No," I told her.

She regarded me carefully. I looked back at her.

"What—?" she began.

"She's mad," Hazel put in from the other side of the room. "She says she's lost her memory and doesn't know us."

"She's been talking about horrid, disgusting things," added one of the others.

"She's got delusions. She thinks she can read and write," Hazel supplemented.

The doctor smiled at that.

"Do you?" she asked me.

"I don't see why not—but it should be easy enough to prove," I replied, brusquely.

She looked startled, a little taken aback, then she recovered her tolerant half-smile.

"All right," she said, humouring me.

She pulled a small note-pad out of her pocket and offered it to me, with a pencil. The pencil felt a little odd in my hand; the fingers did not fall into place readily on it, nevertheless I wrote:

"I'm only too well aware that I have delusions—and that you are part of them."

Hazel tittered as I handed the pad back.

The doctor's jaw did not actually drop, but her smile came right off. She looked at me very hard indeed. The rest of the room, seeing her expression, went quiet, as though I had performed some startling feat of magic. The doctor turned towards Hazel.

"What sort of things has she been telling you?" she inquired.

Hazel hesitated, then she blurted out:

"Horrible things. She's been talking about two human sexes—just as if we were like the animals. It was disgusting!"

The doctor considered a moment, then she told the senior attendant:

"Better get her along to the sick-bay. I'll examine her there."

As she walked off there was a rush of little women to fetch a low trolley from the corner to the side of my couch. A dozen hands assisted me on to it, and then wheeled me briskly away.

"Now," said the doctor grimly, "let's get down to it. Who told you all this stuff about two human sexes? I want her name."

We were alone in a small room with a gold-dotted pink wallpaper. The attendants, after transferring me from the trolley to a couch again, had taken themselves off. The doctor was sitting with a pad on her knee and a pencil at the ready. Her manner was that of an unbluffable inquisitor.

I was not feeling tactful. I told her not to be a fool.

She looked staggered, flushed with anger for a moment, and then took a hold on herself. She went on:

"After you left the Clinic you had your holiday, of course. Now, where did they send you?"

"I don't know," I replied. "All I can tell you is what I told the others—that this hallucination, or delusion, or whatever it is, started in that hospital place you call the Centre."

With resolute patience she said:

"Look here, Orchis. You were perfectly normal when you left here six weeks ago. You went to the Clinic and had your babies in the ordinary way. But between then and now somebody has been filling your head with all this rubbish—and teaching you to read and write, as well. Now you are going to tell me who that somebody was. I warn you you won't get away with this loss of memory nonsense with me. If you are able to remember this nauseating stuff you told the others, then you're able to remember where you got it from."

"Oh, for heaven's sake, talk sense," I told her. She flushed again.

"I can find out from the Clinic where they sent you, and I can find out from the Rest Home who were your chief associates while you were there, but I don't want to waste time following up all your contacts, so I'm asking you to save trouble by telling me now. You might just as well. We don't want to have to make you talk," she concluded, ominously.

I shook my head.

"You're on the wrong track. As far as I am concerned this whole hallucination, including my connection with this Orchis, began somehow at the Centre—how it happened I can't tell you, and what happened to her before that just isn't there to be remembered."

She frowned, obviously disturbed.

"What hallucination?" she inquired, carefully.

"Why this fantastic set-up—and you, too." I waved my hand to include it all. "This revolting great body, all those little women, everything. Obviously it is all some projection of the subconscious—and the state of my subconscious is worrying me, for it's certainly no wish-fulfilment."

She went on staring at me, more worried now.

"Who on earth has been telling you about the subconscious and wish-fulfilments?" she asked uncertainly.

"I don't see why, even in an hallucination, I am expected to be an illiterate moron," I replied.

"But a Mother doesn't know anything about such things. She doesn't need to."

"Listen," I said. "I've told you, as I've told those poor grotesques in the other room, that I am not a Mother. What I am is just an unfortunate M.B. who is having some kind of nightmare."

"M.B.?" she inquired, vaguely.

"Bachelor of Medicine. I practise medicine," I told her.

She went on looking at me curiously. Her eyes wandered over my mountainous form, uncertainly.

"You are claiming to be a doctor?" she said, in an odd voice.

"Colloquially—yes," I agreed.

There was indignation mixed with bewilderment as she protested:

"But this is sheer nonsense! You were brought up and developed to be a Mother. You are a Mother. Just look at you!"

"Yes," I said, bitterly. "Just look at me!"

There was a pause.

"It seems to me," I suggested at last, "that, hallucination or not, we shan't get much further simply by going on accusing one another of talking nonsense. Suppose you explain to me what this place is, and who you think I am. It might jog my memory."

She countered that. "Suppose," she said, "that first you tell me what you can remember. It would give me more idea of what is puzzling you."

"Very well," I agreed, and launched upon a potted history of myself as far as I could recollect it—up to the time, that is to say, when Donald's aircraft crashed.

It was foolish of me to fall for that one. Of course, she had no intention of telling me anything. When she had listened to all I had to say, she went away, leaving me impotently furious.

I waited until the place quietened down. The music had been switched off. An attendant had looked in to inquire, with an air of polishing-off the day's duties, whether there was anything I wanted, and presently there was nothing to be heard. I let a margin of half an hour elapse, and then struggled to get up—taking it by very easy stages this time. The greatest part of the effort was to get on to my feet from a sitting position, but I managed it at the cost of heavy breathing. Presently I crossed to the door, and found it unfastened. I held it a little open, listening. There was no sound of movement in the corridor, so I pulled it wide open, and set out to discover what I could about the place for myself. All the doors of the rooms were shut. Putting my ear close to them I could hear regular, heavy breathing behind some, but there were no other sounds in the stillness. I kept on, turning several corners, until I recognized the front door ahead of me. I tried the latch, and found that it was neither barred nor bolted. I paused again, listening for some moments, and then pulled it open and stepped outside.

The park-like garden stretched out before me, sharp-shadowed in the moonlight. Through the trees to the right was a glint of water, to the left was a house similar to the one behind me, with not a light showing in any of its windows.

I wondered what to do. Trapped in this huge carcase, all but helpless in it, there was very little I could do, but I decided to go on and at least find out what I could while I had the chance. I went forward to the edge of the steps that I had earlier climbed from the ambulance, and started down them cautiously, holding on to the balustrade.

"Mother," said a sharp, incisive voice behind me. "What are you doing?"

I turned and saw one of the little women, her white suit gleaming in the moonlight. She was alone. I made no reply, but took another step down. I could have wept at the outrage of the heavy, ungainly body, and the caution it imposed on me.

"Come back. Come back at once," she told me.

I took no notice. She came pattering down after me and laid hold of my draperies.

"Mother," she said again, "you must come back. You'll catch cold out here."

I started to take another step, and she pulled at the draperies to hold me back. I leant forward against the pull. There was a sharp tearing sound as the material gave. I swung round and lost my balance. The last thing I saw was the rest of the flight of steps coming up to meet me. . . .

As I opened my eyes a voice said:

"That's better, but it was very naughty of you, Mother Orchis. And lucky it wasn't a lot worse. Such a silly thing to do. I'm ashamed of you—really, I am."

My head was aching, and I was exasperated to find that the whole stupid business was still going on; altogether I was in no mood for reproachful drip. I told her to go to hell. Her small face goggled at me for a moment, and then became icily prim. She applied a piece of lint and plaster to the left side of my forehead, in silence, and then departed, stiffly.

Reluctantly, I had to admit to myself that she was perfectly right. What on earth had I been expecting to do—what on earth could I do, encumbered by this horrible mass of flesh? A great surge of loathing for it and a feeling of helpless frustration brought me to the verge of tears again. I longed for my own nice, slim body that pleased me and did what I asked of it. I remembered how Donald had once pointed to a young tree swaying in the wind, and introduced it to me as my twin sister. And only a day or two ago . . .

Then, suddenly, I made a discovery which brought me struggling to sit up. The blank part of my mind had filled up. I could remember everything. . . . The effort made my head throb, so I relaxed and lay back once more, recalling it all, right up to the point where the needle was withdrawn and someone swabbed my arm. . . .

But what had happened after that? Dreams and hallucinations I had expected . . . but not the sharp-focused, detailed sense of reality . . . not this state which was like a nightmare made solid. . . .

What, what in heaven's name, had they done to me . . . ?

I must have fallen asleep again soon, for when I opened my eyes again there was daylight outside, and a covey of little women had arrived to attend to my toilet.

They spread their sheets dexterously and rolled me this way and that with expert technique as they cleaned me up. I suffered their industry patiently, feeling the fresher for it, and glad to discover that the headache had all but gone.

When we were almost at the end of our ablutions there came a peremptory knock, and without invitation two figures, dressed in black uniforms with silver buttons, entered. They were the Amazon type, tall, broad, well set-up, and handsome. The little women dropped everything and fled with squeaks of dismay into the far corner of the room where they cowered in a huddle.

The two gave me the familiar salute. With an odd mixture of decision and deference one of them inquired:

"You are Orchis—Mother Orchis?"

"That's what they're calling me," I admitted.

The girl hesitated, then in a tone rather more pleading than ordering she said:

"I have orders for your arrest, Mother. You will please come with us."

An excited, incredulous twittering broke out among the little women in the corner. The uniformed girl quelled them with a look.

"Get the Mother dressed and make her ready," she commanded.

The little women came out of their corner hesitantly, directing nervous, propitiatory smiles towards the pair. The second one told them briskly, though not altogether unkindly:

"Come along now. Jump to it."

They jumped.

I was almost swathed in my pink draperies again when the doctor strode in. She frowned at the two in uniform.

"What's all this? What are you doing here?" she demanded.

The leader of the two explained.

"Arrest!" exclaimed the doctor. "Arrest a Mother! I never heard such nonsense. What's the charge?"

The uniformed girl said, a little sheepishly:

"She is accused of Reactionism."

The doctor simply stared at her.

"A Reactionist Mother! What'll you people think of next? Go on, get out, both of you."

The young woman protested:

"We have our orders, Doctor."

"Rubbish. There's no authority. Have you ever heard of a Mother being arrested?"

"No, Doctor."

"Well, you aren't going to make a precedent now. Go on."

The uniformed girl hesitated unhappily, then an idea occurred to her.

"If you would let me have a signed refusal to surrender the Mother . . . ?" she suggested helpfully.

When the two had departed, quite satisfied with their piece of paper, the doctor looked at the little women gloomily.

"You can't help tattling, you Servitors, can you? Anything you happen to hear goes through the lot of you like a fire in a cornfield, and makes trouble all round. Well, if I hear any more of this I shall know where it comes from." She turned to me. "And you, Mother Orchis, will in future please restrict yourself to yes-and-no in the hearing of these nattering little pests. I'll see you again shortly. We want to ask you some questions," she added, as she went out, leaving a subdued, industrious silence behind her.

She returned just as the tray which had held my gargantuan breakfast was being removed, and not alone. The four women who accompanied her and looked as normal as herself were followed by a number of little women lugging in chairs which they arranged beside my couch. When they had departed, the five women, all in white overalls, sat down and regarded me as if I were an exhibit. One appeared to be much the same age as the first doctor, two nearer fifty, and one sixty, or more.

"Now, Mother Orchis," said the doctor, with an air of opening the proceedings, "it is quite clear that something highly unusual has taken place. Naturally we are interested to understand just what and, if possible, why. You don't need to worry about those police this morning—it was quite improper of them to come here at all. This is simply an inquiry —a scientific inquiry—to establish what has happened."

"You can't want to understand more than I do," I replied. I looked at them, at the room about me, and finally at my massive prone figure. "I am aware that all this must be an hallucination, but what is troubling me most is that I have always supposed that any hallucination must be deficient in at least one dimension—must lack reality to some of the senses. But this does not. I have all my senses, and can use them. Nothing is insubstantial: I am trapped in flesh that is very palpably too, too solid. The only striking deficiency, so far as I can see, is reason—even symbolic reason."

The four other women stared at me in astonishment. The doctor gave them a sort of now-perhaps-you'll-believe-me glance, and then turned to me again.

"We'll start with a few questions," she said.

"Before you begin," I put in, "I have something to add to what I told you last night. It has come back to me."

"Perhaps the knock when you fell," she suggested, looking at my piece of plaster. "What were you trying to do?"

I ignored that. "I think I'd better tell you the missing part—it might help—a bit, anyway."

"Very well," she agreed. "You told me you were—er—married, and that your—er—husband was killed soon afterwards." She glanced at the others; their blankness of expression was somehow studious. "It was the part after that that was missing," she added.

"Yes," I said. "He was a test-pilot," I explained to them. "It happened six months after we were married—only one month before his contract was due to expire.

"After that, an aunt took me away for some weeks. I don't suppose I'll ever remember that part very well—I—I wasn't noticing anything very much. . . .

"But then I remember waking up one morning and suddenly seeing things differently, and telling myself that I couldn't go on like that. I knew I must have some work, something that would keep me busy.

"Dr. Hellyer, who is in charge of the Wraychester Hospital, where I was working before I married, told me he would be glad to have me with them again. I went back, and worked very hard, so that I did not have much time to think. That would be about eight months ago, now.

"Then one day Dr. Hellyer spoke about a drug that a friend of his had succeeded in synthesizing. I don't think he was really asking for volunteers, but I offered to try it out. From what he said it sounded as if the drug might have some quite important properties. It struck me as a chance to do something useful. Sooner or later, someone would try it, and as I didn't have any ties and didn't care very much what happened, anyway, I thought I might as well be the one to try it."

The spokesman doctor interrupted to ask:

"What was this drug?"

"It's called chuinjuatin," I told her. "Do you know it?"

She shook her head. One of the others put in:

"I've heard the name. What is it?"

"It's a narcotic," I told her. "The original form is in the leaves of a tree that grows chiefly in the South of Venezuela. The tribe of Indians who live there discovered it somehow, like others did quinine, and mescalin. And in much the same way they use it for orgies. Some of them sit and chew the leaves—they have to chew about six ounces of them—and gradually they go into a zombie-like, trance state. It lasts three or four days during which they are quite helpless and incapable of doing the simplest thing for themselves, so that other members of the tribe are appointed to look after them as if they were children, and to guard them.

"It's necessary to guard them because the Indian belief is that chuinjuatin liberates the spirit from the body, setting it free to wander anywhere in space and time, and the guardian's most important job is to see that no other wandering spirit shall slip into the body while the true owner is away. When the subjects recover they claim to have had wonderful mystical experiences. There seem to be no physical ill-effects, and no craving results from it. The mystical experiences, though, are said to be intense, and clearly remembered.

"Dr. Hellyer's friend had tested his synthesized chuinjuatin on a number of laboratory animals and worked out the dosage, and tolerances, and that kind of thing, but what he could not tell, of course, was what validity, if any, the reports of the mystical experiences had. Presumably they were the product of the drug's influence on the nervous system—but whether that effect produced a sensation of pleasure, ecstasy, awe, fear, horror, or any of a dozen more, it was impossible to tell without a human guinea-pig. So that was what I volunteered for."

I stopped. I looked at their serious, puzzled faces, at the billow of pink satin in front of me. . . .

"In fact," I added, "it appears to have produced a combination of the absurd, the incomprehensible, and the grotesque."

They were earnest women, these, not to be side-tracked. They were there to disprove an anomaly—if they could.

"I see," said the spokeswoman with an air of preserving reasonableness, rather than meaning anything. She glanced down at a paper on which she had made a note from time to time.

"Now, can you give us the time and date at which this experiment took place?"

I could, and did, and after that the questions went on and on and on. . . .

The least satisfactory part of it from my point of view was that even though my answers caused them to grow more uncertain of themselves as we went on, they did at least get them; whereas when I put a question it was usually evaded, or answered perfunctorily, as an unimportant digression.

They went on steadily, and only broke off when my next meal arrived. Then they went away, leaving me thankfully in peace—but little the wiser. I half-expected them to return, but when they did not I fell into a doze from which I was awakened by the incursion of a cluster of the little women once more. They brought a trolley with them, and in a short time were wheeling me out of the building on it—but not by the way I had arrived. This time we went down a ramp where another, or the same, pink ambulance waited at the bottom. When they had me safely loaded aboard three of them climbed in, too, to keep me company. They were chattering as they did so, and they kept it up inconsequentially, and almost incomprehensibly, for the whole hour and a half of the journey that ensued.

The countryside differed little from that I had already seen. Once we were outside the gates there were the same tidy fields and standardized farms. The occasional built-up areas were not extensive and consisted of the same types of blocks close by, and we ran on the same, not very good, road surfaces. There were groups of the Amazon types, and, more rarely, individuals, to be seen at work in the fields; the sparse traffic was lorries, large or small, and occasional buses, but with never a private car to be seen. My illusion, I reflected, was remarkably consistent in its details. Not a single group of Amazons, for instance, failed to raise its right hands in friendly, respectful greeting to the pink car.

Once, we crossed a cutting. Looking down from the bridge I thought at first that we were over the dried bed of a canal, but then I noticed a post leaning at a crazy angle among the grass and weeds: most of its attachments had fallen off, but there were enough left to identify it as a railway signal.

We passed through one concentration of identical blocks which was in size, though in no other way, quite a town, and then, two or three miles further on, ran through an ornamental gateway into a kind of park.

In one way it was not unlike the estate we had left, for everything was meticulously tended; the lawns like velvet, the flower-beds vivid with spring blossoms, but it differed essentially in that the buildings were not blocks. They were houses, quite small for the most part, and varied in style, often no larger than roomy cottages. The place had a subduing effect on my small companions; for the first time they left off chattering, and gazed about them with obvious awe.

The driver stopped once to inquire the way of an overalled Amazon who was striding along with a hod on her shoulder. She directed us, and gave me a cheerful, respectful grin through the window, and presently we drew up again in front of a neat little two-storey Regency-style house.

This time there was no trolley. The little women, assisted by the driver, fussed over helping me out, and then half-supported me into the house, in a kind of buttressing formation.

Inside, I was manoeuvred with some difficulty through a door on the left, and found myself in a beautiful room, elegantly decorated and furnished in the period-style of the house. A white-haired woman in a purple silk dress was sitting in a wing-chair beside a wood fire. Both her face and her hands told of considerable age, but she looked at me from keen, lively eyes.

"Welcome, my dear," she said, in a voice which had no trace of the quaver I half-expected.

Her glance went to a chair. Then she looked at me again, and thought better of it.

"I expect you'd be more comfortable on the couch," she suggested.

I regarded the couch—a genuine Georgian piece, I thought —doubtfully.

"Will it stand it?" I wondered.

"Oh, I think so," she said, but not too certainly.

The retinue deposited me there carefully, and stood by, with anxious expressions. When it was clear that, though it creaked, it was probably going to hold, the old lady shooed them away, and rang a little silver bell. A diminutive figure, a perfect parlourmaid three foot ten in height, entered.

"The brown sherry, please, Mildred," instructed the old lady. "You'll take sherry, my dear?" she added to me.

"Y-yes—yes, thank you," I said, faintly. After a pause I added: "You will excuse me, Mrs.—er—Miss—?"

"Oh, I should have introduced myself. My name is Laura —not Miss, or Mrs., just Laura. You, I know, are Orchis— Mother Orchis."

"So they tell me," I owned, distastefully.

We studied one another. For the first time since the hallucination had set in I saw sympathy, even pity, in some-one else's eyes. I looked round the room again, noticing the perfection of details.

"This is—I'm not mad, am I?" I asked.

She shook her head slowly, but before she could reply the miniature parlourmaid returned, bearing a cut-glass decanter and glasses on a silver tray. As she poured out a glass for each of us I saw the old lady glance from her to me and back again, as though comparing us. There was a curious, uninterpretable expression on her face. I made an effort.

"Shouldn't it be madeira?" I suggested.

She looked surprised, and then smiled, and nodded ap-preciatively.

"I think you have accomplished the purpose of this visit in one sentence," she said.

The parlourmaid left, and we raised our glasses. The old lady sipped at hers and then placed it on an occasional table beside her.

"Nevertheless," she went on, "we had better go into it a little more. Did they tell you why they have sent you to me, my dear?"

"No." I shook my head.

"It is because I am a historian," she informed me. "Access to history is a privilege. It is not granted to many of us nowa-days—and then somewhat reluctantly. Fortunately, a feeling that no branches of knowledge should be allowed to perish entirely still exists—though some of them are pursued at the cost of a certain political suspicion." She smiled deprecatingly, and then went on. "So when confirmation is required it is necessary to appeal to a specialist. Did they give you any report on their diagnosis?"

I shook my head again.

"I thought not. So like the profession, isn't it? Well, I'll tell you what they told me on the telephone from the Mother's Home, and we shall have a better idea of what we are about. I was informed that you have been interviewed by several doctors whom you have interested, puzzled—and I suspect, distressed—very much, poor things. None of them has more than a minimum smattering of history, you see. Well, briefly, two of them are of the opinion that you are suffering from delusions of a schizophrenic nature: and three are inclined to think you are a genuine case of projected perception. It is an extremely rare condition. There are not more than three reliably documented cases, and one that is more debatable, they tell me; but of those confirmed two are associated with the drug chuinjuatin, and the third with a drug of very similar properties.

"Now, the majority of three found your answers coherent for the most part, and felt that they were authentically circumstantial. That is to say that nothing you told them conflicted directly with what they know, but, since they know so little outside their professional field, they found a great deal of the rest both hard to believe and impossible to check. Therefore, I, with my better means of checking, have been asked for my opinion."

She paused, and looked me thoughtfully over.

"I rather think," she added, "that this is going to be one of the most curiously interesting things that has happened to me in my quite long life—Your glass is empty, my dear."

"Projected perception," I repeated wonderingly, as I held out my glass. "Now, if *that* were possible—"

"Oh, there's no doubt about the *possibility*. Those three cases I mentioned are fully authenticated."

"It might be that—almost," I admitted. "At least, in some ways it might be—but not in others. There is this nightmare quality. You seem perfectly normal to me, but look at me, myself—and at your little maid! There's certainly an element of delusion. I seem to be here, like this, and talking to you—but it can't really be so, so where am I?"

"I can understand, better than most, I think, how unreal this must seem to you. In fact, I have spent so much of my time in books that it sometimes seems unreal to me—as if I did not quite belong anywhere. Now, tell me, my dear, when were you born?"

I told her. She thought for a moment.

"H'm," she said. "George the Sixth—but you'd not remember the second big war?"

"No," I agreed.

"But you might remember the coronation of the next monarch? Whose was that?"

"Elizabeth—Elizabeth the Second. My mother took me to see the procession," I told her.

"Do you remember anything about it?"

"Not a lot really—except that it rained, nearly all day," I admitted.

We went on like that for a little while, then she smiled, reassuringly.

"Well, I don't think we need any more to establish our point. I've heard about that coronation before—at second-hand. It must have been a wonderful scene in the Abbey." She mused a moment, and gave a little sigh. "You've been very patient with me, my dear. It is only fair that you should have your turn—but I'm afraid you must prepare yourself for some shocks."

"I think I must be inured after my last thirty-six hours—or what has appeared to be thirty-six hours," I told her.

"I doubt it," she said, looking at me seriously.

"Tell me," I asked her. "Please, explain it all—if you can."

"Your glass, my dear. Then I'll get the crux of it over." She poured for each of us, then she asked:

"What strikes you as the oddest feature of your experience, so far?"

I considered. "There's so much—"

"Might it not be that you have not seen a single man?" she suggested.

I thought back. I remembered the wondering tone of one of the Mothers asking: "What is a man?"

"That's certainly one of them," I agreed. "Where are they?"

She shook her head, watching me steadily.

"There aren't any, my dear. Not any more. None at all."

I simply went on staring at her. Her expression was perfectly serious and sympathetic. There was no trace of guile there or deception while I struggled with the idea. At last I managed:

"But—but that's impossible! There must be some somewhere. . . . You couldn't—I mean, how—? I mean . . ." My expostulation trailed off in confusion.

She shook her head.

"I know it must seem impossible to you, Jane—may I call you Jane? But it is so. I am an old woman now, nearly eighty, and in all my long life I have never seen a man—save in old pictures and photographs. Drink your sherry, my dear. It will do you good." She paused. "I'm afraid this upsets you."

I obeyed, too bewildered for further comment at the moment, protesting inwardly, yet not altogether disbelieving, for certainly I had not seen one man, nor sign of any. She went on quietly, giving me time to collect my wits:

"I can understand a little how you must feel. I haven't had to learn all my history entirely from books, you see. When I was a girl, sixteen or seventeen, I used to listen a lot to my grandmother. She was as old then as I am now, but her memory of her youth was still very good. I was able almost to see the places she talked about—but they were part of such a different world that it was difficult for me to understand how she felt. When she spoke about the young man she had been engaged to, tears would roll down her cheeks, even then—not just for him, of course, but for the whole world that she had known as a girl. I was sorry for her, although I could not really understand how she felt—How should I? But now that I am old, too, and have read so much, I am perhaps a little nearer to understanding her feelings, I think." She looked at me curiously. "And you, my dear. Perhaps you, too, were engaged to be married?"

"I was married—for a little time," I told her.

She contemplated that for some seconds, then:

"It must be a very strange experience to be owned," she remarked, reflectively.

"Owned?" I exclaimed, in astonishment.

"Ruled by a husband," she explained, sympathetically.

I stared at her.

"But it—it wasn't like that—it wasn't like that at all," I protested. "It was—" But there I broke off, with tears too close. To steer her away I asked:

"But what happened? What on earth happened to the men?"

"They all died," she told me. "They fell sick. Nobody could do anything for them, so they died. In little more than a year they were all gone—all but a very few."

"But surely—surely everything would collapse?"

"Oh, yes. Very largely it did. It was very bad. There was a dreadful lot of starvation. The industrial parts were the worst hit, of course. In the more backward countries and in rural areas women were able to turn to the land and till it to keep themselves and their children alive, but almost all the large organizations broke down entirely. Transport ceased very soon: petrol ran out, and no coal was being mined. It was quite a dreadful state of affairs because, although there were a great many women, and they had outnumbered the men, in fact, they had only really been important as consumers and spenders of money. So when the crisis came it turned out that scarcely any of them knew how to do any of the important things because they had nearly all been owned by men, and had to lead their lives as pets and parasites."

I started to protest, but her frail hand waved me aside.

"It wasn't their fault—not entirely," she explained. "They were caught up in a process, and everything conspired against their escape. It was a long process, going right back to the eleventh century, in Southern France. The Romantic conception started there as an elegant and amusing fashion for the leisured classes. Gradually, as time went on, it permeated through most levels of society, but it was not until the latter part of the nineteenth century that its commercial possibilities were intelligently perceived, and not until the twentieth that it was really exploited.

"At the beginning of the twentieth century women were starting to have their chance to lead useful, creative, interesting lives. But that did not suit commerce: it needed them much more as mass-consumers than as producers—except on the most routine levels. So Romance was adopted and developed as a weapon against their further progress and to promote consumption, and it was used intensively.

"Women must never for a moment be allowed to forget their sex, and compete as equals. Everything had to have a 'feminine angle' which must be different from the masculine angle, and be dinned in without ceasing. It would have been unpopular for manufacturers actually to issue an order 'back to the kitchen,' but there were other ways. A profession without a difference, called 'housewife,' could be invented. The kitchen could be glorified and made more expensive; it could be made to seem desirable, and it could be shown that the way to realize this heart's desire was through marriage. So the presses turned out, by the hundred thousand a week, journals which concentrated the attention of women ceaselessly and relentlessly upon selling themselves to some man in order that they might achieve some small, uneconomic unit of a home upon which money could be spent.

"Whole trades adopted the romantic approach and the glamour was spread thicker and thicker in the articles, the write-ups, and most of all in the advertisements. Romance found a place in everything that women might buy, from underclothes to motor-bicycles, from 'health' foods to kitchen stoves, from deodorants to foreign travel, until soon they were too bemused to be amused any more.

"The air was filled with frustrated moanings. Women maundered in front of microphones yearning only to 'surrender,' and 'give themselves,' to adore and to be adored. The cinema most of all maintained the propaganda, persuading the main and important part of their audience, which was female, that nothing in life was worth achieving but dewy-eyed passivity in the strong arms of Romance. The pressure became such that the majority of young women spent all their leisure time dreaming of Romance, and the means of securing it. They were brought to a state of honestly believing that to be owned by some man and set down in a little brick box to buy all the things that the manufacturers wanted them to buy would be the highest form of bliss that life could offer."

"But—" I began to protest again. The old lady was now well launched, however, and swept on without a check.

"All this could not help distorting society, of course. The divorce-rate went up. Real life simply could not come near to providing the degree of romantic glamour which was being represented as every girl's proper inheritance. There was probably, in the aggregate, more disappointment, disillusion, and dissatisfaction among women than there had ever been before. Yet, with this ridiculous and ornamented ideal grained-in by unceasing propaganda, what could a conscientious idealist do but take steps to break up the short-weight marriage she had made, and seek elsewhere for the ideal which was hers, she understood, by right?

"It was a wretched state of affairs brought about by deliberately promoted dissatisfactions; a kind of rat-race with, somewhere safely out of reach, the glamourized romantic ideal always luring. Perhaps an exceptional few almost attained it, but, for all except those very few, it was a cruel, tantalizing sham on which they spent themselves, and of course their money, in vain."

This time I did get in my protest.

"But it wasn't like that. Some of what you say may be true—but that's all the superficial part. It didn't feel a bit like the way you put it. I was in it. I *know*."

She shook her head reprovingly.

"There is such a thing as being too close to make a proper evaluation. At a distance we are able to see more clearly. We can perceive it for what it was—a gross and heartless exploitation of the weaker-willed majority. Some women of education and resolution were able to withstand it, of course, but at a cost. There must always be a painful price for resisting majority pressure—even they could not always altogether escape the feeling that they might be wrong, and that the rat-racers were having the better time of it.

"You see, the great hopes for the emancipation of women with which the century had started had been outflanked. Purchasing-power had passed into the hands of the ill-educated and highly suggestible. The desire for Romance is essentially a selfish wish, and when it is encouraged to dominate every other it breaks down all corporate loyalties. The individual woman thus separated from, and yet at the same time thrust into competition with, all other women was almost defenceless; she became the prey of organized suggestion. When it was represented to her that the lack of certain goods or amenities would be fatal to Romance she became alarmed and, thus, eminently exploitable. She could only believe what she was told, and spent a great deal of time worrying about whether she was doing all the right things to encourage Romance. Thus, she became, in a new, a subtler way, more exploited, more dependent, and less creative than she had ever been before."

"Well," I said, "this is the most curiously unrecognizable account of my world that I have ever heard—it's like something copied, but with all the proportions wrong. And as for 'less creative'—well, perhaps families were smaller, but women still went on having babies. The population was still increasing."

The old lady's eyes dwelt on me a moment.

"You are undoubtedly a thought-child of your time, in some ways," she observed. "What makes you think there is anything creative about having babies? Would you call a plant-pot creative because seeds grow in it? It is a mechanical operation—and, like most mechanical operations, is most easily performed by the least intelligent. Now, bringing up a child, educating, helping her to become a person, that is creative. But unfortunately, in the time we are speaking of, women had, in the main, been successfully conditioned into bringing up their daughters to be unintelligent consumers, like themselves."

"But," I said helplessly, "I know the time. It's my time. This is all distorted."

"The perspective of history must be truer," she told me again, unimpressed, and went on: "But if what happened had to happen, then it chose a fortunate time to happen. A hundred years earlier, even fifty years earlier, it would very likely have meant extinction. Fifty years later might easily have been too late—it might have come upon a world in which all women were profitably restricted to domesticity and consumership. Luckily, however, in the middle of the century women were still entering the professions, and by far the greatest number of professional women was to be found in medicine—which is to say that they were only really numerous in, and skilled in, the very profession which immediately became of vital importance if we were to survive at all.

"I have no medical knowledge, so I cannot give you any details of the steps they took. All I can tell you is that there was intensive research on lines which will probably be more obvious to you than they are to me.

"A species, even our species, has great will to survive, and the doctors saw to it that the will had the means of expression. Through all the hunger, and the chaos, and the other privations, babies somehow continued to be born. That had to be. Reconstruction could wait: the priority was the new generation that would help in the reconstruction, and then inherit it. So babies were born: the girl babies lived, the boy babies died. That was distressing, and wasteful, too, and so, presently, only girl babies were born—again, the means by which that could be achieved will be easier for you to understand than for me.

"It is, they tell me, not nearly so remarkable as it would appear at first sight. The locust, it seems, will continue to produce female locusts without male, or any other kind of assistance; the aphis, too, is able to go on breeding alone and in seclusion, certainly for eight generations, perhaps more. So it would be a poor thing if we, with all our knowledge and powers of research to assist us, should find ourselves inferior to the locust and the aphis in this respect, would it not?"

She paused, looking at me somewhat quizzically for my response. Perhaps she expected amazed—or possibly shocked —disbelief. If so, I disappointed her: technical achievements have ceased to arouse simple wonder since atomic physics showed how barriers fall before the pressure of a good brains-team. One can take it that most things are possible: whether they are desirable, or worth doing, is a different matter—and one that seemed to me particularly pertinent to her question. I asked her:

"And what is it that you have achieved?"

"Survival," she said, simply.

"Materially," I agreed. "I suppose you have. But when it has cost all the rest, when love, art, poetry, excitement, and physical joy have all been sacrificed to mere continued existence, what is left but a soulless waste? What reason is there any longer for survival?"

"As to the reason, I don't know—except that survival is a desire common to all species. I am quite sure that the reason for that desire was no clearer in the twentieth century than it is now. But, for the rest, why should you assume that they are gone. Did not Sappho write poetry? And your assumption that the possession of a soul depends upon a duality of sexes surprises me: it has so often been held that the two are in some sort of conflict, has it not?"

"As a historian who must have studied men, women, and motives you should have taken my meaning better," I told her.

She shook her head, with reproof. "You are so much the conditioned product of your age, my dear. They told you, on all levels, from the works of Freud to that of the most nugatory magazines for women, that it was sex, civilized into romantic love, that made the world go round—and you believed them. But the world continues to go round for others, too—for the insects, the fish, the birds, the animals—and how much do you suppose they know of romantic love, even in their brief mating-seasons? They hoodwinked you, my dear. Between them they channelled your interests and ambitions along courses that were socially convenient, economically profitable, and almost harmless."

I shook my head.

"I just don't believe it. Oh, yes, you know something of my world—from the outside. But you don't understand it, or feel it."

"That's your conditioning, my dear," she told me, calmly.

Her repeated assumption irritated me. I asked:

"Suppose I were to believe what you say, what is it, then, that does make the world go round?"

"That's simple, my dear. It is the will to power. We have that as babies; we have it still in old age. It occurs in men and women alike. It is more fundamental, and more desirable, than sex; I tell you, you were misled—exploited, sublimated for economic convenience.

"After the disease had struck, women ceased, for the first time in history, to be an exploited class. Without male rulers to confuse and divert them they began to perceive that all true power resides in the female principle. The male had served only one brief useful purpose; for the rest of his life he was a painful and costly parasite.

"As they became aware of power, the doctors grasped it. In twenty years they were in full control. With them were the few women engineers, architects, lawyers, administrators, some teachers, and so on, but it was the doctors who held the keys of life and death. The future was in their hands and, as things began gradually to revive, they, together with the other professions, remained the dominant class and became known as the Doctorate. It assumed authority; it made the laws; it enforced them.

"There was opposition, of course. Neither the memory of the old days, nor the effect of twenty years of lawlessness, could be wiped out at once, but the doctors had the whip-hand—any woman who wanted a child had to come to them, and they saw to it that she was satisfactorily settled in a community. The roving gangs dwindled away, and gradually order was restored.

"Later on, they faced better organized opposition. There was a party which contended that the disease which had struck down the men had run its course, and the balance could, and should, be restored—they were known as Re-actionists, and they became an embarrassment.

"Most of the Council of the Doctorate still had clear memories of a system which used every weakness of women, and had been no more than a more civilized culmination of their exploitation through the ages. They remembered how they themselves had only grudgingly been allowed to qualify for their careers. They were now in command: they felt no obligation to surrender their power and authority, and eventually, no doubt, their freedom to a creature whom they had proved to be biologically, and in all other ways, expendable. They refused unanimously to take a step that would lead to corporate suicide, and the Reactionists were proscribed as a subversive criminal organization.

"That, however, was just a palliative. It quickly became clear that they were attacking a symptom and neglecting the cause. The Council was driven to realize that it had an unbalanced society at its hands—a society that was capable of continuity, but was in structure, you might say, little more than the residue of a vanished form. It could not continue in that truncated shape and, as long as it tried to, disaffection would increase. Therefore, if power were to become stable, a new form suitable to the circumstances must be found.

"In deciding the shape it should take, the natural tendencies of the little-educated and uneducated woman were carefully considered—such qualities as her feeling for hierarchical principles and her disposition to respect artificial distinctions. You will no doubt recollect that in your own time any fool of a woman whose husband was ennobled or honoured at once acquired increased respect and envy from other women though she remained the same fool; and also, that any gathering or society of unoccupied women would soon become obsessionally enmeshed in the creation and preservation of social distinctions. Allied to this is the high value they usually place upon a feeling of security. Important, too, is the capacity for devoted self-sacrifice, and slavery to conscience within the canons of any local convention. We are naturally very biddable creatures. Most of us are happiest when we are being orthodox, however odd our customs may appear to an outsider; the difficulty in handling us lies chiefly in establishing the required standards of orthodoxy.

"Obviously, the broad outline of a system which was going to stand any chance of success would have to provide scope for these and other characteristic traits. It must be a scheme where the interplay of forces would preserve equilibrium and respect for authority. The details of such an organization, however, were less easy to determine.

"An extensive study of social forms and orders was undertaken, but for several years every plan put forward was rejected as in some way unsuitable. The architecture of that finally chosen was said, though I do not know with how much truth, to have been inspired by the Bible—a book at that time still unprohibited, and the source of much unrest. I am told that it ran something like: 'Go to the ant, thou sluggard; consider her ways.'

"'The Council appears to have felt that this advice, suitably modified, could be expected to lead to a state of affairs which would provide most of the requisite characteristics.

"A four-class system was chosen as the basis, and strong differentiations were gradually introduced. These, now that they have become well established, greatly help to ensure stability: there is scope for ambition within one's class, but none for passing from one class to another. Thus, we have the Doctorate—the educated ruling-classes, fifty per cent of whom are actually of the medical profession. The Mothers, whose title is self-explanatory. The Servitors, who are numerous and, for psychological reasons, small. The Workers, who are physically and muscularly strong, to do the heavier work. All the three lower classes respect the authority of the Doctorate. Both the employed classes revere the Mothers. The Servitors consider themselves more favoured in their tasks than the Workers; and the Workers tend to regard the puniness of the Servitors with a semi-affectionate contempt.

"So you see a balance has been struck, and though it works somewhat crudely as yet, no doubt it will improve. It seems likely, for instance, that it would be advantageous to introduce sub-divisions into the Servitor class before long, and the police are thought by some to be put at a disadvantage by having no more than a little education to distinguish them from the ordinary Worker. . . .'"

She went on explaining with increasing detail while the enormity of the whole process gradually grew upon me.

"Ants!" I broke in, suddenly. "The ant-nest! You've taken *that* for your model?"

She looked surprised, either at my tone, or the fact that what she was saying had taken so long to register.

"And why not?" she asked. "Surely it is one of the most enduring social patterns that nature has evolved—though of course some adaptation—"

"You're—are you telling me that only the Mothers have children?" I demanded.

"Oh, members of the Doctorate do, too, when they wish," she assured me.

"But—but."

"The Council decides the ratios," she went on to explain. "The doctors at the clinic examine the babies and allocate them suitably to the different classes. After that, of course, it is just a matter of seeing to their specialized feeding, glandular control, and proper training."

"But," I objected wildly, "what's it for? Where's the sense in it? What's the good of being alive, like that?"

"Well, what is the sense in being alive? You tell me," she suggested.

"But we're meant to love and be loved, to have babies we love by people we love."

"There's your conditioning again; glorifying and romanticizing primitive animalism. Surely you consider that we are superior to the animals?"

"Of course I do, but—"

"Love, you say, but what can you know of the love there can be between mother and daughter when there are no men to introduce jealousy? Do you know of any purer sentiment than the love of a girl for her little sisters?"

"But you don't understand," I protested again. "How should you understand a love that colours the whole world? How it centres in your heart and reaches out from there to pervade your whole being, how it can affect everything you are, everything you touch, everything you hear. . . . It can hurt dreadfully, I know, oh, I know, but it can run like sunlight in your veins. . . . It can make you a garden out of a slum; brocade out of rags; music out of speaking voice. It can show you a whole universe in someone else's eyes. Oh, you don't understand . . . you don't know . . . you can't. . . . Oh, Donald, darling, how can I show her what she's never even guessed at . . . ?"

There was an uncertain pause, but presently she said:

"Naturally, in your form of society it was necessary for you to be given such a conditioned reaction, but you can scarcely expect us to surrender our freedom, to connive at our own re-subjection by calling our oppressors into existence again."

"Oh, you won't understand. It was only the more stupid men and women who were continually at war with one another. Lots of us were complementary. We were pairs who formed units."

She smiled. "My dear, either you are surprisingly ill-informed on your own period, or else the stupidity you speak of was astonishingly dominant. Neither as myself, nor as a historian, can I consider that we should be justified in resurrecting such a state of affairs. A primitive stage of our development has now given way to a civilized era. Woman, who is the vessel of life, had the misfortune to find man necessary for a time, but now she does so no longer. Are you suggesting that such a useless and dangerous encumbrance ought to be preserved, out of sheer sentimentality? I will admit that we have lost some minor conveniences—you will have noticed, I expect, that we are less inventive mechanically, and tend to copy the patterns we have inherited; but that troubles us very little; our interests lie not in the inorganic, but in the organic and the sentient. Perhaps men could show us how to travel twice as fast, or how to fly to the moon, or how to kill more people more quickly; but it does not seem to us that such kinds of knowledge would be good payment for re-enslaving ourselves. No, our kind of world suits us better—all of us except a few Reactionists. You have seen our Servitors. They are a little timid in manner, perhaps, but are they oppressed, or sad? Don't they chatter among themselves as brightly and perkily as sparrows? And the Workers—those you called the Amazons—don't they look strong, healthy, and cheerful?"

"But you're robbing them all—robbing them of their birthright."

"You mustn't give me cant, my dear. Did not your social system conspire to rob a woman of her 'birthright' unless she married? You not only let her know it, but socially you rubbed it in: here, our Servitors and Workers do not know it, and they are not worried by a sense of inadequacy. Motherhood is the function of the Mothers, and understood as such."

I shook my head. "Nevertheless, they are being robbed. A woman has a right to love—"

For once she was a little impatient as she cut me short.

"You keep repeating to me the propaganda of your age. The love you talk about, my dear, existed in your little sheltered part of the world by polite and profitable convention. You were scarcely ever allowed to see its other face, unglamourized by Romance. You were never openly bought and sold, like livestock; you never had to sell yourself to the first comer in order to live; you did not happen to be one of the women who through the centuries screamed in agony and suffered and died under invaders in a sacked city—nor were you ever flung into a pit of fire to be saved from them; you were never compelled to suttee upon your dead husband's pyre; you did not have to spend your whole life imprisoned in a harem; you were never part of the cargo of a slave-ship; you never retained your own life only at the pleasure of your lord and master. . . .

"That is the other side—the age-long side. There is going to be no more of such things. They are finished at last. Dare you suggest that we should call them back, to suffer them all again?"

"But most of these things had already gone," I protested. "The world was getting better."

"Was it?" she said. "I wonder if the women of Berlin thought so when it fell? Was it, indeed?—or was it on the edge of a new barbarism?"

"But if you can only get rid of evil by throwing out the good, too, what is there left?"

"There is a great deal. Man was only a means to an end. We needed him in order to have babies. The rest of his vitality accounted for all the misery in the world. We are a great deal better off without him."

"So you really consider that you've improved on nature?"

"Tcha!" she said, impatient with my tone. "Civilization is improvement on nature. Would you want to live in a cave and have most of your babies die in infancy?"

"There are some things, some fundamental things—" I began, but she checked me, holding up her hand for silence.

Outside, the long shadows had crept across the lawns. In the evening quiet I could hear a choir of women's voices singing some little distance away. We listened for some minutes until the song was finished.

"Beautiful!" said the old lady. "Could angels themselves sing more sweetly? They sound happy enough, don't they? Our own lovely children—two of my granddaughters are there among them. They are happy, and they've reason to be happy: they're not growing up into a world where they must gamble on the goodwill of some man to keep them; they'll never need to be servile before a lord and master; they'll never stand in danger of rape and butchery, either. Listen to them!"

Another song had started and came lilting lightly to us out of the dusk.

"Why are you crying?" the old lady asked me as it ended.

"I know it's stupid—I don't really believe any of this is what it seems to be—so I suppose I'm crying for all you would have lost if it were true," I told her. "There should be lovers out there under the trees; they should be listening hand in hand to that song while they watch the moon rise. But there are no lovers now, there won't be any more. . . ." I looked back at her.

"Did you ever read the lines: 'Full many a flower is born to blush unseen, and waste its sweetness on the desert air'? Can't you feel the forlornness of this world you've made? Do you *really* not understand?" I asked.

"I know you've only seen a little of us, but do you not begin to understand what it can be like when women are no longer forced to fight one another for the favours of men?" she countered.

We talked on while the dusk gave way to darkness and the lights of other houses started to twinkle through the trees. Her reading had been wide. It had given her even an affection for some periods of the past, but her approval of her own era was unshaken. She felt no aridity in it. Always it was my 'conditioning' which prevented me from seeing that the golden age of woman had begun at last.

"You cling to too many myths," she told me. "You speak of a full life, and your instance is some unfortunate woman hugging her chains in a suburban villa. Full life, fiddlesticks! But it was convenient for the traders that she could be made to think so. A truly full life would be an exceedingly short one, in any form of society."

And so on. . . .

At length, the little parlourmaid reappeared to say that my attendants were ready to leave when it should be convenient. But there was one thing I very much wanted to know before I left. I put the question to the old lady.

"Please tell me. How did it—how could it—happen?"

"Simply by accident, my dear—though it was the kind of accident that was entirely the product of its time. A piece of research which showed unexpected, secondary results, that's all."

"But how?"

"Rather curiously—almost irrelevantly, you might say. Did you ever hear of a man called Perrigan?"

"Perrigan?" I repeated. "I don't think so; it's an uncommon name."

"It became very commonly known indeed," she assured me. "Doctor Perrigan was a biologist, and his concern was the extermination of rats—particularly the brown rat, which used to do a great deal of expensive damage.

"His approach to the problem was to find a disease which would attack them fatally. In order to produce it he took as his basis a virus infection often fatal to rabbits—or, rather, a group of virus infections that were highly selective, and also unstable since they were highly liable to mutation. Indeed, there was so much variation in the strains that when infection of rabbits in Australia was tried, it was only at the sixth attempt that it was successful; all the earlier strains died out as the rabbits developed immunity. It was tried in other places, too, though with indifferent success until a still more effective strain was started in France, and ran through the rabbit population of Europe.

"Well, taking some of these viruses as a basis, Perrigan induced new mutations by irradiation and other means, and succeeded in producing a variant that would attack rats. That was not enough, however, and he continued his work until he had a strain that had enough of its ancestral selectivity to attack only the brown rat, and with great virulence.

"In that way he settled the question of a long-standing

pest, for there are no brown rats now. But something went amiss. It is still an open question whether the successful virus mutated again, or whether one of his earlier experimental viruses was accidentally liberated by escaped 'carrier' rats, but that's academic. The important thing is that somehow a strain capable of attacking human beings got loose, and that it was already widely disseminated before it was traced —also, that once it was free, it spread with devastating speed; too fast for any effective steps to be taken to check it.

"The majority of women were found to be immune; and of the ten per cent or so whom it attacked over eight per cent recovered. Among men, however, there was almost no immunity, and the few recoveries were only partial. A few men were preserved by the most elaborate precautions, but they could not be kept confined for ever, and in the end the virus, which had a remarkable capacity for dormancy, got them, too."

Inevitably several questions of professional interest occurred to me, but for an answer she shook her head.

"I'm afraid I can't help you there. Possibly the medical people will be willing to explain," she said, but her expression was doubtful.

I manœuvred myself into a sitting position on the side of the couch.

"I see," I said. "Just an accident—yes, I suppose one could scarcely think of it happening any other way."

"Unless," she remarked, "unless one were to look upon it as divine intervention."

"Isn't that a little impious?"

"I was thinking of the Death of the Firstborn," she said, reflectively.

There did not seem to be an immediate answer to that. Instead, I asked:

"Can you honestly tell me that you never have the feeling that you are living in a dreary kind of nightmare?"

"Never," she said. "There was a nightmare—but it's over now. Listen!"

The voices of the choir, reinforced now by an orchestra, reached us distantly out of the darkened garden. No, they were not dreary: they even sounded almost exultant—but then, poor things, how were they to understand . . . ?

My attendants arrived and helped me to my feet. I thanked the old lady for her patience with me and her kindness. But she shook her head.

"My dear, it is I who am indebted to you. In a short time I have learnt more about the conditioning of women in a mixed society than all my books have been able to show me in the rest of my long life. I hope, my dear, that the doctors will find some way of enabling you to forget it and live happily here with us."

At the door I paused and turned, still helpfully shored up by my attendants.

"Laura," I said, using her name for the first time, "so many of your arguments are right—yet, over all, you're, oh, so wrong. Did you never read of lovers? Did you never, as a girl, sigh for a Romeo who would say: 'It is the east, and Laura is the sun!'?"

"I think not. Though I have read the play. A pretty, idealized tale—I wonder how much heartbreak it has given to how many would-be Juliets? But I would set a question against yours, my dear Jane. Did you ever see Goya's cycle of pictures called 'The Horrors of War'?"

The pink car did not return me to the 'Home'. Our destination turned out to be a more austere and hospital-like building where I was fussed into bed in a room alone. In the morning, after my massive breakfast, three new doctors visited me. Their manner was more social than professional, and we chatted amiably for half an hour. They had evidently been fully informed on my conversation with the old lady, and they were not averse to answering my questions. Indeed, they found some amusement in many of them, though I found none, for there was nothing consolingly vague in what they told me—it all sounded too disturbingly practicable, once the technique had been worked out. At the end of that time, however, their mood changed. One of them, with an air of getting down to business, said:

"You will understand that you present us with a problem. Your fellow Mothers, of course, are scarcely susceptible to

Reactionist disaffection—though you have in quite a short time managed to disgust and bewilder them considerably—but on others less stable your influence might be more serious. It is not just a matter of what you may say; your difference from the rest is implicit in your whole attitude. You cannot help that, and, frankly, we do not see how you, as a woman of education, could possibly adapt yourself to the placid, unthinking acceptance that is expected of a Mother. You would quickly feel frustrated beyond endurance. Furthermore, it is clear that the conditioning you have had under your system prevents you from feeling any goodwill towards ours."

I took that straight; simply as a judgment without bias. Moreover, I could not dispute it. The prospect of spending the rest of my life in pink, scented, soft-musicked illiteracy, interrupted, one gathered, only by the production of quadruplet daughters at regular intervals, would certainly have me violently unhinged in a very short time.

"And so—what?" I asked. "Can you reduce this great carcase to normal shape and size?"

She shook her head. "I imagine not—though I don't know that it has ever been attempted. But even if it were possible, you would be just as much of a misfit in the Doctorate—and far more of a liability as a Reactionist influence."

I could understand that, too.

"What, then?" I inquired.

She hesitated, then she said gently:

"The only practicable proposal we can make is that you should agree to a hypnotic treatment which will remove your memory."

As the meaning of that came home to me I had to fight off a rush of panic. After all, I told myself, they were being reasonable with me. I must do my best to respond sensibly. Nevertheless, some minutes must have passed before I answered, unsteadily.

"You are asking me to commit suicide. My mind is my memories: they are me. If I lose them I shall die, just as surely as if you were to kill my—this body."

They did not dispute that. How could they?

There is just one thing that makes my life worth living—knowing that you loved me, my sweet, sweet Donald. It is only in my memory that you live now. If you ever leave there you will die again—and for ever.

"No!" I told them. "No! No!"

At intervals during the day small servitors staggered in under the weight of my meals. In between their visits I had only my thoughts to occupy me, and they were not good company.

"Frankly," one of the doctors had put it to me, not unsympathetically, "we can see no alternative. For years after it happened the annual figures of mental breakdowns were our greatest worry. Even though the women then could keep themselves fully occupied with the tremendous amount of work that had to be done, so many of them could not adjust. And we can't even offer you work."

I knew that it was a fair warning she was giving me—and I knew that, unless the hallucination which seemed to grow more real all the time could soon be induced to dissolve, I was trapped.

During the long day and the following night I tried my hardest to get back to the objectivity I had managed earlier, but I failed. The whole dialectic was too strong for me now; my senses too consciously aware of my surroundings; the air of consequence and coherence too convincingly persistent. . . .

When they had let me have twenty-four hours to think it over, the same trio visited me again.

"I think," I told them, "that I understand better now. What you are offering me is painless oblivion, in place of a breakdown followed by oblivion—and you see no other choice."

"We don't," admitted the spokeswoman, and the other two nodded. "But, of course, for the hypnosis we shall need your co-operation."

"I realize that," I told her, "and I also see now that in the circumstances it would be obstinately futile to withhold it. So I—I—yes, I'm willing to give it—but on one condition."

They looked at me questioningly.

"It is this," I explained, "that you will try one other course first. I want you to give me an injection of chuinjuatin. I want it in precisely the same strength as I had it before—I can tell you the dose.

"You see, whether this is an intense hallucination, or whether it is some kind of projection which makes it seem very similar, it must have something to do with that drug. I'm sure it must—nothing remotely like this has ever happened to me before. So, I thought that if I could repeat the condition—or, would you say, believe myself to be repeating the condition?—there may be just a chance . . . I don't know. It may be simply silly . . . but even if nothing comes of it, it can't make things worse in any way now, can it? So, if you will let me try it . . . ?"

The three of them considered for some moments.

"I can see no reason why not . . ." said one.

The spokeswoman nodded.

"I shouldn't think there'll be any difficulty with authorization in the circumstances," she agreed. "If you want to try, well, it's fair to let you, but—I'd not count on it too much. . . ."

In the afternoon half a dozen small servitors arrived, bustling round, making me and the room ready, with anxious industry. Presently there came one more, scarcely tall enough to see over the trolley of bottles, trays, and phials which she pushed to my bedside.

The three doctors entered together. One of the little servitors began rolling up my sleeve. The doctor who had done most of the talking looked at me, kindly, but seriously.

"This is a sheer gamble, you know that?" she said.

"I know. But it's my only chance. I'm willing to take it."

She nodded, picked up the syringe, and charged it while the little servitor swabbed my monstrous arm. She approached the bedside, and hesitated.

"Go on," I told her. "What is there for me here, anyway?"

She nodded, and pressed in the needle. . . .

Now, I have written the foregoing for a purpose. I shall deposit it with my bank, where it will remain unread unless it should be needed.

I have spoken of it to no one. The report on the effect of chuinjuatin—the one that I made to Dr. Hellyer where I described my sensation as simply one of floating in space—was false. The foregoing was my true experience.

I concealed it because after I came round, when I found that I was back in my own body in my normal world, the experience haunted me as vividly as if it had been actuality. The details were too sharp, too vivid, for me to get them out of my mind. It overhung me all the time, like a threat. It would not leave me alone. . . .

I did not dare to tell Dr. Hellyer how it worried me—he would have put me under treatment. If my other friends did not take it seriously enough to recommend treatment, too, then they would have laughed over it, and amused themselves at my expense interpreting the symbolism. So I kept it to myself.

As I went over parts of it again and again in detail, I grew angry with myself for not asking the old lady for more facts, things like dates, and details that could be verified. If, for instance, the thing should, by her account, have started two or three years ago, then the whole sense of threat would fall to pieces: it would all be discredited. But it had not occurred to me to ask that crucial question. . . . And then, as I went on thinking about it, I remembered that there was one, just one, piece of information that I could check, and I made inquiries. I wish now that I had not, but I felt forced to. . . .

So I have discovered that:

There *is* a Dr. Perrigan, he *is* a biologist, he does work with rabbits and rats. . . .

He is quite well known in his field. He has published papers on pest-control in a number of journals. It is no secret that he is evolving new strains of myxomatosis to attack rats; indeed, he has already developed a group of them and calls them mucosimorbus, though he has not yet succeeded in making them either stable or selective enough for general use. . . .

But I had never heard of this man or his work until his name was mentioned by the old lady in my 'hallucination'. . . .

I have given a great deal of thought to this whole matter. What sort of experience is it that I have recorded above? If it should be a kind of pre-vision of an inevitable, predestined future, then nothing anyone could do would change it. But this does not seem to me to make sense: it is what has happened, and is happening now, that determines the future. Therefore, there must be a great number of *possible* futures, each a possible consequence of what is being done now. It seems to me that under chuinjuatin I saw one of those futures. . . .

It was, I think, a warning of what may happen—unless it is prevented. . . .

The whole idea is so repulsive and misconceived, it amounts to such a monstrous aberration of the normal course, that failure to heed the warning would be neglect of duty to one's kind.

I shall, therefore, on my own responsibility and without taking any other person into my confidence, do my best to ensure that such a state as I have described *cannot* come about.

Should it happen that any other person is unjustly accused of doing, or of assisting me to do, what I intend to do, this document must stand in his defence. That is why I have written it.

It is my own unaided decision that Dr. Perrigan must not be permitted to continue his work.

(Signed) JANE WATERLEIGH.

The solicitor stared at the signature for some moments; then he nodded.

"And so," he said, "she then took her car and drove over to Perrigan's—with this tragic result.

"From the little I do know of her, I'd say that she probably did her best to persuade him to give up his work—though she can scarcely have expected any success with that. It is difficult to imagine a man who would be willing to give up the work of years on account of what must sound to him like a sort of gipsy's warning. So, clearly, she went prepared to fall back on direct action, if necessary. It looks as if the police are quite right when they suppose her to have shot him deliberately; but not so right when they suppose that she burnt the place down to hide evidence of the crime. The statement makes it pretty obvious that her main intention in doing that was to wipe out Perrigan's work."

He shook his head. "Poor girl! There's a clear conviction

of duty in her last page or two: the sort of simplified clarity that drives martyrs on, regardless of consequences. She has never denied that she did it. What she wouldn't tell the police is why she did it."

He paused again, before he added: "Anyway, thank goodness for this document. It ought at least to save her life. I should be very surprised indeed if a plea of insanity could fail, backed up by this." He tapped the pile of manuscript with his finger. "It's a lucky thing she put off her intention of taking it to her bank."

Dr. Hellyer's face was lined and worried.

"I blame myself most bitterly for the whole thing," he said. "I never ought to have let her try the damned drug in the first place, but I thought she was over the shock of her husband's death. She was trying to keep her time fully occupied, and she was anxious to volunteer. You've met her enough to know how purposeful she can be. She saw it as a chance to contribute something to medical knowledge—which it was, of course. But I ought to have been more careful, and I ought to have seen afterwards that there was something wrong. The real responsibility for this thing runs right back to me."

"H'm," said the solicitor. "Putting that forward as a main line of defence isn't going to do you a lot of good professionally, you know, Hellyer."

"Possibly not. I can look after that when we come to it. The point is that I hold a responsibility for her as a member of my staff, if for no other reason. It can't be denied that, if I had refused her offer to take part in the experiment, this would not have happened. Therefore it seems to me that we ought to be able to argue a state of temporary insanity; that the balance of her mind was disturbed by the effects of the drug which I administered. And if we can get that as a verdict it will result in detention at a mental hospital for observation and treatment—perhaps quite a short spell of treatment."

"I can't say. We can certainly put it up to counsel and see what he thinks of it."

"It's valid, too," Hellyer persisted. "People like Jane don't do murder if they are in their right minds, not unless they're really in a corner, then they do it more cleverly. Certainly they don't murder perfect strangers. Clearly, the drug caused an hallucination sufficiently vivid to confuse her to a point where she was unable to make a proper distinction between the actual and the hypothetical. She got into a state where she believed the mirage was real, and acted accordingly."

"Yes. Yes, I suppose one might put it that way," agreed the solicitor. He looked down again at the pile of paper before him. "The whole account is, of course, unreasonable," he said, "and yet it is pervaded throughout with such an air of reasonableness. I wonder . . ." He paused pensively, and went on: "This expendability of the male, Hellyer. She doesn't seem to find it so much incredible, as undesirable. That seems odd in itself to a layman who takes the natural order for granted, but would you, as a medical scientist, say it was—well, not impossible, in theory?"

Dr. Hellyer frowned.

"That's very much the kind of question one wants more notice of. It would be very rash to proclaim it *impossible*. Considering it purely as an abstract problem, I can see two or three lines of approach. . . . Of course, if an utterly improbable situation were to arise calling for intensive research— research, that is, on the sort of scale they tackled the atom— well, who can tell . . . ?" He shrugged.

The solicitor nodded again.

"That's just what I was getting at," he observed. "Basically it is only just such a little way off the beam; quite near enough to possibility to be faintly disturbing. Mind you, as far as the defence is concerned, her air of thorough conviction, taken in conjunction with the near-plausibility of the thing, will probably help. But as far as I am concerned it is just that nearness that is enough to make me a trifle uneasy."

The doctor looked at him rather sharply.

"Oh, come! Really now! A hard-boiled solicitor, too! Don't tell me you're going in for fantasy-building. Anyway, if you are, you'll have to conjure up another one. If Jane, poor girl, has settled one thing, it is that there's no future in this particular fantasy. Perrigan's finished with, and all his work's gone up in smoke."

"H'm," said the solicitor again. "All the same, it would be more satisfactory if we knew of some way other than this"— he tapped the pile of papers—"some other way in which she is likely to have acquired a knowledge of Perrigan and his work. There is, as far as one knows, no other way in which he can have come into her orbit at all—unless, perhaps, she takes an interest in veterinary subjects?"

"She doesn't. I'm sure of that," Hellyer told him, shaking his head.

"Well, that, then, remains one slightly disturbing aspect. And there is another. You'll think it foolish of me, I'm sure —and no doubt time will prove you right to do so—but I have to admit I'd be feeling easier in my mind if Jane had been just a bit more thorough in her inquiries before she went into action."

"Meaning—?" asked Dr. Hellyer, looking puzzled.

"Only that she does not seem to have found out that there is a son. But there is, you see. He appears to have taken quite a close interest in his father's work, and is determined that it shan't be wasted. In fact he has already announced that he will do his best to carry it on with the very few specimens that were saved from the fire. . . .

"Laudably filial, no doubt. All the same it does disturb me a little to find that he, also, happens to be D.Sc., a biochemist; and that, very naturally, his name, too, is Perrigan. . . ."

The Dream

BOY IN DARKNESS

by Mervyn Peake

The ceremonies were over for the day. The Boy was tired out. Ritual, like a senseless chariot, had rolled its wheels—and the natural life of the day was bruised and crushed.

Lord of a tower'd tract, he had no option but to be at the beck and call of those officials whose duty it was to advise and guide him. To lead him hither to thither through the mazes of his adumbrate home. To celebrate, from day to day, in remote ceremonies the meaning of which had long been forgotten.

The traditional birthday gifts had been proffered him on the traditional gold tray by the master of the Ritual. Long lines of servants, knee-deep in water, passed before him as he sat hour after hour by the margin of the gnat-haunted lake. The whole occasion had been one to try the patience of an equable adult and for a child it was hell.

This, the Boy's birthday, was the second of the two most arduous days of the whole year. On the previous day he had been involved in a long march up the steep flanks of a hill to a plantation where it had been necessary for him to plant the fourteenth of a group of ash trees, for to-day he was fourteen years old. It was no mere formality, for he had no one to help him as he worked, in a long grey cloak and a hat rather like a dunce's cap. On his return journey down the steep hill he had stumbled and fallen, bruising his knee and cutting his hand so that, by the time he was at last alone in his small room overlooking the red-stone square, he was in a frame of mind quite savage in its resentment.

But now, on the evening of his second day, his birthday, the day of so many idiotic ceremonies that his brain throbbed with incongruous images and his body with fatigue, he lay upon his bed with his eyes closed.

After resting for some while he opened one of his eyes at what sounded like a moth fluttering against the window. He could see nothing, however, and was about to close his eyes again when he caught sight of that ochre-coloured and familiar patch of mildew that stretched across the ceiling like an island.

He had stared many times at this same mildew-island with its inlets and its bays; its coves and the long curious isthmus that joined the southern to the northern masses. He knew by heart the tapering peninsula that ended in a narrowing chain of islets like a string of discoloured beads: He knew the lakes and the rivers and he had many a time brought imaginary ships to anchor in hazardous harbours, or stood them off when the seas ran high where they rocked in his mind and set new courses for yet other lands.

But to-day he was too irritable to make-believe and the only thing he stared at was a fly that was moving slowly across the island.

"An explorer, I suppose," muttered the Boy to himself—and as he muttered there came before his eyes the hated outline of the mountain and the fourteen stupid ash-trees, and the damnable presents that were handed to him on the golden tray, only to be returned to the vaults twelve hours later, and he saw a hundred familiar faces, every one of which reminded him of some ritual duty so that he beat his hands upon the bed shouting, "No! No! No!" and sobbed until the fly on the mildew-island had crossed from east to west and was now following the coastline as though it had no wish to venture out across the ceiling-sea.

Only a little part of his consciousness was taken up with watching the fly but that little was identifying itself with the insect so that the Boy became dimly aware of *exploration* as something more than a word or a sound of a word, as something solitary and mutinous. And then it came, all at once, the first flicker of imperative rebellion, not against any one particular person but against the eternal round of deadly symbolism.

He longed (he knew it now) to turn his anger into action —to make his escape from the gaols of precedent; to make a bid if not for final freedom then at least for a day. For a day. For one tremendous day of insurrection.

Insurrection! It was indeed nothing less. Was he truly contemplating so radical a step? Had he forgotten the pledges he had made as a child and on a thousand subsequent occasions? The solemn oaths that bound him with chords of allegiance, to his home.

And then the whisper that breathed between his shoulder-blades as though urging him to fly—that whisper that was growing in volume and intensity. "Just for a little while," it said. "After all you are only a boy. What kind of fun are you having?" He heaved himself over in bed and gave out a great yell.

"O damn the Castle! Damn the Laws! Damn everything!" He sat bolt upright on the edge of his bed. His heart was beating fast and thick. A soft golden light was pouring through his window in a kind of haze and through the haze could be seen the double line of banners that shook along the roof-tops in his honour.

He took a deep breath and looked slowly around the room and was then suddenly arrested by a near-by face. It stared at him fiercely. It was a young face despite the fact that the forehead was puckered up in a deep frown. Hanging on a cord around the neck was a bunch of turkey feathers.

It was by those feathers that he knew that he was looking at himself and he turned away from the mirror, tearing, as he did so, the absurd trophy that hung around his neck. It was for him to wear the feathers all night before handing them back on the following morning to the Hereditary Master of the Quills. As it was, he jumped from the bed, tore off the rotting relic and trampled upon it.

Then came the upsurge again! The thrill and speculation of escape. Of escape to where? And when? When should it be? "Why, now! now! now!" came the voice. "Be up and be gone. What are you waiting for?"

But the Boy who was so fretful to be gone had another side. Something more icy, so that while his body trembled and cried, his mind was not so childish. Whether to make his bid for freedom at speed and by daylight or during the long hours of darkness was not easy to decide. At first it seemed the obvious choice was to wait for the sun to sink and, taking the night for his ally, to beat his way into the fastness while the core of the castle lay heavy with sleep and smothered in ivy like a bitter veil. To creep through the labyrinthine lanes that he knew so well and out into the draughty starlit spaces and on . . . and on.

But in spite of the obvious and immediate advantages of making his escape by night yet there was the dire peril of his becoming irrevocably lost or falling into the hands of evil forces.

Fourteen years of age, he had had many opportunities to test his courage in the tortuous castle and he had on many an occasion been terrified, not only by the silences and glooms of the night but by a sense of being watched, almost as though the castle itself, or the spirit of the ancient place moved with him as he moved, stopped when he stopped; for ever breathing at his shoulder-blades and taking note of every move he made.

Remembering these times when he had lost himself he could not but realize how much more frightening it would be for him to be alone in the darkness of a district alien to his life, a place remote from the kernel of the Castle where, although he detested many of the inhabitants, he was at least among his own kind. For there can be a need for hateful things, and a hatred of what is, in a strange way, loved. And so a child flies to what it recognizes for recognition's sake. But to be alone in a land where nothing can be recognized, that is what he feared, and that is what he longed for. For what is exploration without peril?

But no. He would not start away in darkness. That would be madness. He would start a little before dawn with most of the Castle asleep, and he would run through the half-light, and race the sun—he on the ground and the sun in the air— the two of them, alone.

But how to bear the cold, slow-footed night—the interminable night that lay ahead. Sleep seemed impossible, though sleep he needed. He slid off his bed and walked rapidly to the window. The sun was not far above the notched horizon, and all things swam in a pale translucency. But not for long. The gentle vista took, all of a sudden, another aspect. Towers that a moment ago had been ethereal, and all but floated in the golden air, had now become, through loss of the sun's late beams, like black and carious teeth.

A shudder ran over the darkened terrain and the first of the night-owls floated noiselessly past the window. Far below him a voice was shouting. It was too far away for the words to be decipherable but not too far for them to be coloured with anger. Another voice took up the argument. Titus leaned over the window-sill and stared down vertically. The antagonists were the size of sun-flower seeds. A bell began to chime, and then another and then a swarm of bells. Harsh bells and mellow ones: bells of many metals and many ages: bells of fear and bells of anger: gay bells and mournful: thick bells and clear bells . . . the flat and the resonant, the exultant and the sad. For a few moments they filled the air together; a murmuration; with a clamour of tongues: that spread their echoes over the great shell of the castle like a shawl of metal. Then one by one the tumult weakened and scores of bells fell away until there was nothing but an uneasy silence, until, infinitely far away, a slow and husky voice stumbled its way over the roof-tops and the Boy at the window heard the last of the thick notes die into silence.

For a moment he was caught up in the familiar splendour of it all. He never tired of the bells. Then just as he was about to turn from the window there came another peal of such urgency as to make him frown, for he could not think what it could mean. Then came another peal and then another and after the fourteenth had ended it was clear that he was being saluted. He had forgotten for a little while his status, only to be reminded with a jolt. He could not escape his birthright. It might be thought to have such deference shown him could not but give pleasure to a boy. But it was not so in the case of the young earl. His whole life had been swamped with ceremony, and his happiest moments were when he was alone.

Alone. Alone? That meant away. Away, but where? That lay beyond his powers to imagine.

Beyond the window the night was heavy with its own darkness, only interrupted by the pin-points of light that flickered along the backbone of that same steep-sided mountain he had climbed and in whose flank he had planted the fourteenth ash-tree. These distant sparks or embers burned not only on the mountain but along the periphery of a great circle—and it was in obedience to the beckoning bonfires that crowds were beginning to form in a score of courtyards.

For to-night was the night of high barbecue and within

a little while, long lines of retainers would be on their way to one or other section of the circle. The Castle would empty itself and men on horseback, men on foot, mules and carriages, and all sorts of vehicles would set out. And, leaping to and fro in anticipation, a crowd of urchins would scream and fight, their cries like the cries of starlings.

It was these cries that now rose through the dark air that upset whatever plans he had formed and whatever wisdom the Boy possessed. They were shrill with the excitement of childhood, and standing at the window he suddenly and without conscious thought knew, positively, knew absolutely, that he must escape now: now in the thick and turmoil of it all. Now, while ritual rang with bells and bonfires: now, on the crest of decision.

He was agile, and he needed to be, for the course he set for himself was hazardous. This was no mere matter of rushing down long flights of stairs. This was at once something faster and more secretive.

For many years he had, out of sheer inquisitiveness, pried here and there among the dust-filled rooms of his seemingly endless home until he had discovered a dozen ways of reaching the ground without touching the main stairways and without being seen. If there was ever a time for him to use his knowledge this was it, so at the T-shaped ending of the forty-foot corridor along which he was racing he neither turned right to the northern, nor left to the southern stairs that swept down, down, down, in scything curves of worm-riddled wood, but instead he jumped for a small glassless window immediately overhead and, catching hold of a short stub-end of rope that protruded from the window-base, he hauled himself up and through—

Stretching before him was a long attic, the beams of which were so low that to make progress there was no question of merely stooping, let alone walking upright. The only method was to lie flat and wriggle on knees and elbows. This could be a wearisome business, for the attic was extensive, but the Boy had reduced the process to such a rhythmic science that to see him would be like watching a mechanical toy.

At the far end there was a trapdoor which, when pulled open on its hinge, disclosed, from above, a long drop to an outstretched blanket like a huge blue hammock. The corners were tied with cord attached to the low beams; the belly of the blanket swung free of the ground.

Within a few moments he was through the trapdoor and had bounced from the blanket on to the floor like an acrobat. This room must once have been cared for. There were signs of faded elegance, but the high, square room now breathed a forlorn and dismal air.

Had it not been that the window of this room was thrown wide to the night, the Boy might by now have been finding it impossible to see his hand before his face. But the window made a rectangle of dark grey that appeared to be let in to the surrounding blackness of the room.

Moving rapidly to the window, he edged his way over the sill and out into the open air and now began the long swarm down a hundred feet of tough grey rope.

After what seemed to be a long while he reached another small window in the enormous expanse of the wall and he wriggled his way through this disused opening and left the long rope swinging aimlessly.

Now he was on some kind of a landing and a moment later he was pounding his way down flight after flight of stairs until he came to a derelict hall.

At the Boy's approach a husky scuffling sound suggested that a number of little creatures had been startled and were making for their lairs.

The floor of the one-time hall was not a floor in the ordinary sense, for the floorboards had long since rotted away and where they should have been the grass grew luxuriantly and a host of molehills filled the place as though it were an ancient burial ground.

For a few moments, not knowing why, he stood still and listened. It was not the kind of place for racing through, for there is a certain grandeur in decay and in the stillness, which slows the footsteps.

When he halted there was no sound at all, but now, as from another world, he heard the far-away voices of children, so faint that at first he thought it was the sound of a beetle rubbing its thighs together.

He turned to his left where there was once the door and

at the far end of a corridor he saw the small square of light no bigger than a finger-nail. He began to make his way down this corridor, but there was a different air about him now. The madness had gone out of his flight. He was moving gingerly.

For there was a light at the far end of the corridor. A dull red glow suggesting sundown? What could it be? The sun had sunk long ago.

Then came far, shrill voices again, this time louder, although no single word could be recognized: and then he realized what was happening.

The children of the castle were at large. It was their night of nights with torches blazing: Their voices grew louder as the Boy advanced, until he saw them through the archway and they covered the ground, an army of wild children, so that he found no difficulty in slipping unobserved into their teeming ranks. The torches flared in the voice-filled night and the light of the torches shone on their wet foreheads and flashed in their eyes. And the Boy marched with them until, realizing that they were making for the traditional Torch Mountain, he gradually dropped behind and, choosing his moment, he sheered off at a junction where the trees grew thickly among high mounds of masonry and he was, once again, alone.

By now he was several miles from the Castle itself and deep into less obvious territory. Less obvious but still recognizable by reason of the occasional idiosyncrasy of stone or metal. A shape protruding from a wall, a jag or jutting that rose to the brink of memory.

So the Boy moved on and on, catching glimpse after glimpse of half-remembered, half-forgotten shapes; but these shapes that clung to his mind because of their peculiarities (a stain across the ground the shape of a three-fingered hand, or the spiral movement of a branch above his head) became, as he proceeded, further and further apart and the time came when, for a quarter of an hour, he was alone with no mark or sign to guide him.

It was as though he had been deserted by the outriders of his memory and an uprush of fear flowed over him like an icy wave.

He turned in the darkness, this way and that, flashing his torch along the endless walk to set the webs of spiders in a blaze or blind a lizard on its ferny shelf. There was no one about, and the only sound was the slow drip of water and the occasional rustling of ivy.

Then he remembered his motive, his reason for being where he was: lost in a fastness; he remembered the endless ritual of his primordial home: he remembered his anger and how he was determined to defy the sacred laws of his family and his kingdom, and he stamped his feet on the ground for, in spite of all this, he was frightened at what he had done and frightened of the night and he began to run, his footsteps sounding loud upon the stones until he came to a great stretch of land where only a few trees grew with their arms flung out as though in exasperation, and as he ran the moon slid out of the thick clouds and he saw ahead of him a river.

A river! What river could this be? There was, it is true, a river that wound about his home, but this was something quite different—a wide, sluggish waterway with no trees upon its banks, a featureless, slow-moving stretch of sullen water with the bilious moonlight glowering on its back.

He had come to a halt on seeing this, and as he stood he felt the darkness close in behind him so that he turned his head and saw the dogs.

Out of nowhere, it seemed, these hounds had gathered themselves together. Never in his life had the Boy seen so many. There had been, of course, the scavengers, flitting from time to time down the corridors of his home, hugging the walls, baring their fangs—the shadow—the yelp, and a scuffle in the dark—and then the silence again. But this was something very different, where the dogs seemed to be a part of the day and night, cocksure of themselves, their lean, grey heads held high in the air. Hounds out of somewhere else— they lived in forsaken halls and lay down all together in a single blot of darkness—or in the glaring noon they covered the stone floors of ruined cloisters as thick on the ground as autumn leaves.

They gathered themselves in a half-moon and, without touching him, seemed yet to urge him eastwards to the bank of the great river.

The breath from their lungs was deep and fierce, but there seemed to be no immediate menace in it. Not by the merest graze did the fanged horde of these hounds touch the Boy, who was yet impelled to go forward inch by inch until he stood on the brink of the great waterway where a shallow skiff lay moored. With the breathing of the beasts all about him he stepped down into the skiff and, with shaking hands, untied the painter. Then grabbing a kind of punting pole he pushed off into the sluggish stream. But he was not free of the dogs who, leaping into the water, surrounded him so that a great flotilla of canine heads bobbed up and down in the moon-glazed water, their ears pointed, their fangs bright in the light of the moon. But it was their eyes that were appalling, for they were that kind of bright and acid yellow that allowed no other colour alongside and, if a colour can have any moral value, was ineradicably wicked.

Fearful as he was, and amazed as he was to find himself in this strange predicament, yet, in spite of the pack, he was less ill with terror than he might have been, utterly alone. The dogs were unwittingly his companions. They, unlike the iron and the stone, were alive and had in common with him the throb of life in their breasts and he threw up a prayer of gladness as he dug the long pole into the mud of the riverbed.

But he was deadly tired, and his weariness joined with the easing of his loneliness to the point where he all but fell asleep. But he kept his eyelids open and the time came when he reached the opposite bank and stepped out over the side into the warm moonlit water and the hounds turned about and drifted away like a dark carpet.

So he was alone again and his terror might have returned had he not been so tired. As it was, he crawled up a shallow bank until he reached dry ground and then, curling up, he fell incontinently asleep.

How long he slept was difficult for him to estimate, but when he woke it was broad daylight, and as he raised himself on one arm he knew that all was ill. This was not the air of his own country. This was foreign air. He looked about and nothing was familiar. He had known on the previous night that he was lost, but this was another kind of sensation, for it seemed that he was not only far from home but that some new quality hovered between him and the sun. It was not, not that something had gone that in his heart of hearts he wanted back, but that something lay ahead of him that he had no wish to meet. What it could be he had no inkling. All he knew was that it would be different. The sun upon his face felt hot and very dry. His sight appeared to be keener than ever, as though a film had been taken away from his eyes and an odour quite unlike any other began to force itself upon his notice.

It was not unpleasant in itself. In fact there was a trace of sweetness inextricably tangled with the menace.

He turned his back upon the wide and creeping river and, leaving the skiff in the shallow water, clenched his hands together. Then he started to walk with quick, nervous steps towards the low hills that lay over the skyline where walls and rooftops were intermixed with trees and the branches of trees.

As he went on there were indications, at first hardly recognizable, that he was on evil ground. Tinges of glaucous colour, now here, now there, appeared before his eyes. They lay thinly like snail-slime, or glistened from the occasional stone or along a blade of grass or spread like a blush over the ground.

But a blush that was grey. A wet and slippery thing that moved hither and thither over the foreign ground. It shone with a horrible light upon the dark earth—and then was gone and the reverse took its place, for the blush was now the dark and slithering thing and the terrain all about it shone like the skin of a leper.

The Boy turned his head from something he could not understand in order to rest his eyes upon—the river, for even that ghastly waterway was some kind of a comfort, for it was in the past and the past can do no further harm. It had done him none. As for the dogs, not one had harmed him, though the panting of their lungs was frightful. It was their eyes that had been devilish.

There was no such colour now that the daylight had returned. The sun, for all its strength, gave out the kind of light that sucked out every hue. For the moon to have done this would have been in keeping with the baleful light she casts, but in her case something of the reverse had happened, for the eyes were lemon-yellow.

But when the Boy turned to the waterway behind him, as though for comfort, he saw how changed it was. Whatever it had been like on that previous night, it was no friend to him now. The water under the sun's rays was like grey oil that heaved as though with a voluptuous sickness. The Boy turned his head back again and ran a little way as though from some vile beast.

In contrast to the oleaginous river the harsh outline of the wooded hill was crusty like bread, and with never a glance behind him he made in that direction.

It was now many hours since he had last had a meal and his hunger was becoming almost unbearable. The level ground was thick with dust.

Perhaps it was this soft white dust that killed the sound of approaching footsteps: for the Boy had no suspicion that something was approaching him. It was not until a waft of sour breath touched him that he started and leapt to one side and faced the newcomer.

The face was unlike anything the boy had ever seen before. It was too big. Too long. Too shaggy. Too massive altogether for decency, for there is a kind of malproportion that is best kept away from public view.

The figure who stood so upright (even to the extent of appearing to lean backward a little as though recoiling) was dressed in a dark and ridiculously voluminous suit of some thick material. The starched cuffs, which had once been white, were so long and loose that they completely covered up his hands.

He wore no hat, but a mass of dusty little curls covered his cranium and spread down the back of his neck.

The protruding and osseous temples appeared to be thrusting their way through the wig-like hair. The eyes were horribly paled and glassy, with such small pupils as to be virtually invisible.

If the Boy was not able to take in everything at a glance, he was at least able to know that he was facing something that could never have been discovered in the precincts of his home. It was in some way of another order. And yet what was it that made this gentleman so different? His hair was curly and dusty. This was somehow revolting but there was nothing monstrous about it. The head was long and huge. But why should that, in itself, be repellent, or impossible? The eyes were pale, and almost pupil-less, but what of that? The pupil was there, though tiny, and there was obviously no need for its enlargement.

The Boy dropped his eyes for the merest fraction of a second, for one of the feet had raised itself into the air and was scratching the thigh of the opposite leg with horrid deliberation.

The Boy shuddered a little, but why? The gentleman had done nothing wrong.

Yet all was different. All was wrong, and the Boy, whose heart was beating thick and fast, watched the newcomer with apprehension. It was then that the long hirsute head lowered itself and rolled a little from side to side.

"What do you want?" said the Boy. "Who are you?"

The gentleman ceased to swing his head about and looked fixedly at the Boy, baring his teeth in a smile.

"Who are you?" the Boy repeated. "What is your name?"

The black-coated figure leaned back in his tracks, so that there was something pompous about him. But the smile was still spread across his face like a dazzling wound.

"I am Goat," he said, and the noise of it came thickly from between his shining teeth. "I have come to welcome you, child. Yes . . . yes . . . to welcome you. . . ."

The man who called himself Goat then took a sidelong step towards the Boy—a vile and furtive step which, when it had reached its limit of extension, began to oscillate a hoof-like shoe that, as it dropped the white dust to and fro in an almost prudish way, revealed a central crack along the welt. The Boy retreated involuntarily but could not help staring at the beastly terminal as he did so. This cracked foot was not of a kind of thing that any right-minded man would care to exhibit to a stranger. But the Goat did nothing but shift it to and fro, only ceasing from time to time to watch the soft sand as it poured back from the split and on to the ground again.

"Child," he said (still scraping the sand about), "wince not away from me. Shall I carry you?"

"No!" cried the Boy, in so quick and loud a voice that the smile of the Goat went off and on again like a light.

"Very well," said the Goat, "then you must walk."

"Where to?" said the Boy. "I think I would like to go home."

"That is just where you are going, child," said the Goat, and then in a kind of ruminative afterthought he repeated the words. "That is just where you are going."

"To the Castle?" said the Boy. "To my room? Where I can rest?"

"Oh, no, not there," said the Goat. "Nothing to do with any *castle*."

"Where I can rest," repeated the Boy, "and have something to eat. I am very hungry," and then a fit of temper ran through him and he shouted at the black-suited, long-headed Goat, "Hungry! Hungry!" and he stamped his foot on the ground.

"There will be a banquet for you," said the Goat. "It will be held in the Iron Room. You are the first."

"The first what?" said the Boy.

"The first visitor. You are what we have been waiting for so long. Would you like to stroke my beard?"

"No," said Titus. "Get away from me."

"Now that's a cruel thing to say to me," said the Goat, "especially as I'm the kindest one of all. You wait till you see the others. You are just what they want."

Then the Goat began to laugh and his large, loose white cuffs flipped to and fro as he beat his arms at his sides.

"I tell you what," it said. "If you tell me things, then I'll tell you things. How would you like that?" The Goat leaned forward and gazed at the Boy with his empty-looking eyes.

"I don't know what you mean," whispered the Boy, "but find me food or I will never do anything for you, I will hate you even more—and I will kill you—yes, kill you because of my hunger. Get me bread! Get me bread!"

"Bread is not good enough for you," said the Goat. "Oh, dear, no. What you need are things like figs and rushes." He bent over the Boy and his black greasy coat smelt faintly of ammonia. "And another thing you need is . . ."

He did not finish his sentence because the boy gave at the knees and slumped to the ground in a dead faint.

The long hairy jaws of the Goat fell open like those of a mechanical toy, and dropping to his knees he shook his head in an inane way, so that the dry dust that covered the curls on his head rose and drifted away in the joyless sunlight. When the Goat had stared for some time he rose to his feet and sidled away for perhaps twenty or thirty paces, looking over his shoulder every so often to make sure that he was not mistaken. But no. There was the Boy where he left him, motionless as ever. Then the Goat turned in his tracks and gazed at the rough horizon where trees and hills were knotted together in a long string. And as he watched he saw, a long way off, something no larger than an insect running. It seemed at times to be on all fours, but then to change to run almost upright, and the effect upon the Goat was immediate.

A gleam of dull light that had both fear and vengeance in it flickered for a moment across the blank of the Goat's eyes and he began to paw the ground, sending up spurts of white gravelly dust. Then he returned at a trot to the Boy, and, lifting him with an ease that suggested that a terrible strength lay hidden within the loose ammonia-smelling jacket, he slung him like a sack over his shoulder and then began to make for the horizon with a kind of awkward sideways run.

And as he ran on and on over the white dust he muttered to himself.

"First of all our sovereign lord of the white head, the Lamb, and there is only the Lamb, for he is the heart of life and love, and that is true because he *tells* us so. So first of all I call to him through darkness. To be received. And I will be rewarded, it may be, by the soft vice in his voice. And that is true because he told me so. And it is very secret and Hyena must not know. . . . Hyena must not know . . . because I found him on my very own. So Hyena must not see me or the creature . . . the hungry creature . . . the creature we have waited for so long. . . . My present to the Lamb . . . the Lamb, his master . . . lord of the snow-white . . . the very Lamb."

As he ran, in that sideways manner, he continued to pour

out the thoughts as they bubbled up confusedly at the brink of his poor, deluded brain. His power of running seemed to have no bounds. He did not pant or gasp for air. Only once did he stop and that was in order to scratch his head deep down in the undergrowth of his dusty, verminous curls where his forehead and his crown were itching as though his head was on fire. To do this he had to place the Boy on the ground and it was at about this point that a few grass-blades could be seen pushing up through the dust. The wooded hills were by now appreciably closer, and as the Goat scratched his head and while this operation was sending up clouds of dust that hung in the air, the creature who had been observed in the distance once again made its appearance.

But the Goat had his head turned away from that direction and it was the Hyena who, loping back from some wicked-ness or other, suddenly saw his colleague and froze on the instant where he stood, like a thing of metal, its animal ears pricked forward sharply. Its protruding eyes were filled with the Goat and with something else. What was that shape that lay on the dust at the Goat's feet?

For some while he could not make it out, even with his acute and comprehensive eyesight—but then, as the Goat turned to the Boy, shaking down his long cuffs still further as he did so, and, as he picked the Boy up with his forearm and slung him over his back, Hyena could see the outline of a human face, and as he saw this he began to tremble with so terrible a vitality of the blood that the distant Goat stared about him as though there was a change in the weather, or as though the sky had changed colour.

Feeling the change but not knowing what to do about it, for nothing was to be seen or heard, the Goat began to run again, his black cloak-like coat flapping out behind him and the Boy over his shoulder.

Hyena watched carefully, for the Goat was by now within a few hundred yards of the periphery of the wooded hills. Once in the shadow of the trees it was not easy to track down a foe, or find a friend.

But Hyena, although noting with care the direction of the Goat's progress, was nevertheless pretty sure of his route and his destination. For, as Hyena knew, the Goat was a lick-spittle and a toady, who would never dare to risk the wrath of the Lamb. That is where he would be going. To the heart of the terrain where deep in the silence stood the Ware-houses.

So the Hyena waited a little while and, as he watched, the air around him was loud with the sound of bones being cracked, for Hyena was fond of marrow and kept a quiverful of bones in his pocket. His jaws were very powerful, and as he crunched the muscles could be seen working between his ears and his jaw; and this was made all the more apparent by the fact that Hyena, in contrast to the Goat, was some-thing of a dandy, shaving himself with a cut-throat razor with great care every five or six hours. For the bristles on his jowl were tough and rapid and had to be dealt with. His long forearms were another matter. Thickly covered with a brindled growth, they were something to be proud of, and for this reason Hyena was never to be seen in a jacket. The shirt he wore was cut off very short in the sleeves so that his long, spotted arms could be readily appreciated. But by far the most impressive thing about him was his mane that billowed down through a vent in the shirt between the shoulder-blades. His trousered legs were very narrow and very short, so that his back, as a result, was at a very steep incline. So much so, in fact, that he was often to be seen dropping his long-armed forelegs to the ground.

There was about him something very foul. As with the Goat it was difficult to pin this foulness down to any partic-ular feature, horrid enough as that may have been. But there was a kind of menace all the same about Hyena; a menace very different from the vague beastliness of the Goat. Less unctuous, less stupid, less dirty than the Goat, but bloodier, crueller and with a fiercer blood-drive and, for all the ease with which the Goat had shouldered the Boy, a bestial strength of quite a different order. That clean white shirt, wide open at the front, disclosed a hinterland, black and rocklike.

Bobbing about in the half-darkness was a blood-ruby, that hung and smouldered on a big golden chain.

There he stood, at midday, at the edge of the wood, his eyes fixed upon Goat with the Boy on his shoulders. And as

he stood there he cocked his head on one side and at the same
time brought out of his trousers pocket a great knuckle of
bone, the size of a doornob and, nuzzling this seemingly
intractable thing between his eye-teeth, he cracked it open as
though it were an egg-shell.

Then he drew on a pair of yellow gloves (his eyes never
leaving the Goat) and, unhooking his walking-cane from the
branch of a nearby tree, he suddenly turned and dived into
the shadows of the forest trees that stood motionless like some
kind of ominous curtain.

Once among the trees and the little hills he tucked the
cane, for safe keeping, through the hairs of his shaggy mane
and, dropping his forelegs to the ground, began to gallop
through the semi-darkness as though he were an animal. And
as he ran he began to laugh, mournfully at first, until this
unhappy sound gave place by degrees to another kind of
beastliness. There is a kind of laughter that sickens the soul.
Laughter when it is out of control: when it screams and
stamps its feet, and sets the bells jangling in the next town.
Laughter in all its ignorance and its cruelty. Laughter with
the seed of Satan in it. It tramples upon shrines; the belly-
roarer. It roars, it yells, it is delirious: and yet it is as cold
as ice. It has no humour. It is naked noise and naked malice,
and such was Hyena.

For Hyena had such raw vitality of the blood, such brutal
ebullience, that as he ran over the ferns and grasses a kind
of throbbing went with him. An almost audible thing, in the
profound silence of the forest. For there was a sense of silence
in spite of the monstrous and idiotic laughter, a silence more
deadly than any long-drawn stillness, for every fresh burst
was like a knife wound, every silence a new nullity.

But by degrees the laughter grew less and less, until he
came to a clearing among the trees and there was no noise at
all. He had travelled very fast and was not surprised to find
that he had outstripped the Goat, for he was confident, nor
was he wrong, that the Goat would be making for the Mines.
Certain that he would not have long to wait, Hyena sat upright on a boulder and began to readjust his clothes, darting
a glance from time to time at a gap in the trees.

As nothing appeared for some while, Hyena began to study

his long, powerful and brindled forearms and seemed pleased
with what he saw, for groups of muscles moved across his
shaven cheeks and the corner of his mouth lifted into what
might have been either a smile or a snarl and a moment later
there was a sound of something moving among the branches
and there, all at once, was the Goat.

The Boy, still in a faint, hung limply over the black-clothed
shoulder. For some while the Goat stood quite still, not because he had seen Hyena, but because this glade, or clearing,
was like a stage or a landmark in his progress, and he paused,
involuntarily, to rest. The sunlight fell upon his knobbly forehead. The long, dirty, white cuffs swung to and fro, annihi-
lating whatever hands he possessed. His long jacket, so black
in the semi-darkness, had about it, in the sunlight, a greenish
tinge that suggested decay.

Hyena, who had been sitting motionless on his boulder,
now got to his feet and a bestial strength was redolent in every
movement he made. But the Goat had begun to shift the Boy
on to his other shoulder and Hyena was still unobserved,
until a crack like a rifle-shot caused the Goat to wheel about
on his cracked shoes and at the same moment to drop his
precious burden.

It was a sound he recognized, that whip-crack, that gun-
shot, for it was, along with the cracking and crunching, as
much a part of Hyena's existence as the mane on the back
of his spotted forearms.

"Fool of a fool!" cried Hyena. "Clot! Lout! And Damnable Goat! Come here before I add another bump to your
dirty brow! And bring that bundle with you," he said,
pointing at the heap on the forest floor. He did not know
any more than the Goat that the Boy was watching them
through half-closed eyes.

The Goat did a sideways shuffle and then displayed his
teeth in the most fatuous of dazzling smiles.

"Hyena, dear," he said. "How well you are looking!
Quite your own self again, I shouldn't wonder. Bless your
long forearms and your splendid mane."

"Forget my forearms, Goat! Fetch me the bundle."

"And so I will," said the Goat. "Indeed and of course."
And the Goat drew the swathes of his filthy jacket about him

as though he were cold, and sidled away to where the Boy lay seemingly inert.

"Is he dead?" said Hyena. "If so, I'll crack your leg-bone. He must be living when we take him there."

"We take him there? Is that what you said?" said the Goat. "By the splendour of your mane, Hyena, dear, you are despising me. It is *I* who found him. *I*, Capricorn, the Goat . . . if you'll forgive me. I shall take him alone."

Then the vile blood leapt in the veins of the brute. With one great spring, the sinewy Hyena was upon the Goat and was holding him down. The surge of sheer, malicious, uncontrollable vitality shook his frame as though to shake it to pieces, so that while Hyena held the Goat helpless on its back (for his hands gripped the poor creature by its shoulders) he trod savagely to and fro along the length of his victim, his cruel hands remaining where they were.

The Boy lay quietly watching the brutal scene. His soul retched as he watched and it was all he could do to stop himself getting to his feet and running. But he knew that he had no chance against the two of them. Even were he to have been strong and well, he could never have escaped from the bounding Hyena, whose body appeared to contain the spleen and energy of Satan himself.

As it was, lying alone on the wide floor of a foreign world, his limbs as heavy as lead, the very idea of escape was ludicrous.

But he had not let the moments go by without some reward. He had learned from broken sentences that there was Another. Another creature—a creature vague and tenuous in the Boy's mind, but something that assumed some kind of power, not only over the Goat, but the impetuous Hyena also—and perhaps over others.

The Goat, muscular as he was, gave in entirely to Hyena, for he knew the brindled beast of old, and to what cruelties he could resort were he to have put up any resistance. As it was, the Hyena sprang away from the bruised Goat and rearranged the folds of his white shirt. The eyes in his long, lean face shone with a disgusting light.

"Has your foul carcase had enough of it? Eh? Why he puts up with you is beyond me."

"Because he's blind," whispered the Goat. "You ought to know *that*, Hyena, dear. Ah me, how rough you are."

"Rough? That was nothing! Why—"

"No, no, my dear. There's no need to tell me. I know you are stronger than I am. So there is little I can do."

"There's nothing you can do," said Hyena. "Repeat it after me."

"What?" said the Goat, who was by now sitting up. "I don't quite understand you, Hyena, my love."

"If you call me your love again, I'll skin you," said Hyena, and he brought out a long, slim blade. The sunbeams danced upon it.

"Yes . . . yes . . . I've seen it before," said the Goat. "I know all about that sort of thing. After all, you have bullied me for years and years, haven't you?" and he flashed his fatuous smile so that his teeth looked like a graveyard. Never was there a mouth so empty of mirth. He turned from the Hyena and made his way again to where the Boy lay silently, but, before he reached the seemingly insensate bundle, he turned and cried:

"Oh, but it's shameful. It was I who found him—found him alone in the white dust, and it was I who crept up to him and surprised him. It was all my doing and now I must share it. O Hyena! Hyena! You are more brutal than I and you must have your way."

"And so I shall. Never fear," said the Hyena, cracking a fresh bone between his teeth and spitting out a cloud of white powder.

"But oh, it's the glory that I need," said the Goat. "It's the glory of it."

"Ah," said Hyena. "You are lucky that I let you come at all—you Knobhead."

At this pleasantry the Goat merely scratched himself, but with such force that the dust arose from every corner of his anatomy so that he was for a few moments quite invisible in a small column of white dust. Then he turned his baleful, all-but-pupil-less pale eyes upon his companion and then with his inimitable sideways trot he approached the Boy—but before he had reached him Hyena came hurtling through the air and was already sitting very upright by the Boy's side.

"You see my mane, don't you, cockroach?"

"Of course I do," said the Goat. "It needs oiling!"

"Silence!" said Hyena. "Do what I tell you!"

"What would that be, Hyena, dear?"

"Plait my mane!"

"Oh, no!" cried Goat. "Not now . . ."

"Plait my mane!"

"What then, Hyena?"

"Plait the six ropes of it!"

"What for, my dear?"

"For to tie him to me with. I shall take him on my back to the Lamb. That will please the Lamb. So plait my mane and bind him to the plaits. Then I can run, you shuffling sod! Run as only I can run. I can run like the wind I can, like the black winds from the wastelands. I am the fastest in the world. Faster than my fastest foe. As for my strength— the very finest lions vomit and slink away. Who else has arms like mine. Even the very Lamb admired them long ago . . . in the days when he could see me. Oh, Fool of a fool! you sicken me. Plait my mane. My black mane! What are you waiting for?"

"I found him in the dust-lands by myself, and now you . . ."

But the Goat was interrupted by a movement in the tail of his eye and, turning his dusty head quickly in the direction of the Boy, he saw him get to his feet. At the same moment Hyena ceased in his crunching of a marrowy knuckle and for a few moments the three of them stood quite still. Around them the leaves of the trees fluttered but made no sound. There were no birds. There was nothing, it seemed, that was alive. The ground itself had a deadness about it. No insects made their way from grass blade to grass blade, or from stone to stone. The sun shone down in a dead, flat heat.

The Boy, weak as he was, and frightened as he was, had nevertheless been listening to the conversation, and he had gathered one or two thoughts together, and it was he who broke the stillness with his young voice.

"In the name of the Blind Lamb," he cried. "Salutations to you both." He turned to Hyena. "May the spots upon your magnificent forearms never grow faint with the lashing of the winter rains or black in the summer sun."

He paused. His heart was beating violently. His taut limbs trembled. But he felt the silence of their concentration grow; so intently did they stare at him.

He knew he must go on.

"And what a mane! How proud and arrogant are the hairs on it! With what a black, torrential surge do they break through your snow-white shirt. Let it never be rearranged or altered in any way, this wrath of a mane, save to be combed by moonlight when the owls are hunting. O splendid creature. And what a jaw for cracking. Indeed you must be proud of the power in your tendons and the granite of your teeth."

The Boy turned his head to the Goat and drew in a deep shuddering breath. "Ah, Goat," he said. "We have met before. I remember you so well. Was it in this world or the last? I remember the amplitude of your smile and the serene detachment of your gaze. But, oh, what was it about your walk? What was it? There was something that was so very personal about it. Would you walk for me, Mr. Goat? Out of the kindness of your heart. Would you walk so far as that tree and back? Will you? So that I can remember?"

For a moment or two there was no sound. It seemed that Goat and Hyena were rooted where they stood. They had never heard such eloquence. They had never been so amazed. The bundle of weakness over whose prostrate body they had been arguing was now standing between them.

Then the air became suddenly mournful as a far-away howl was heard, but only for a moment, for it then turned into a scream of penetrating laughter—mirthless, hideous. The whole vast, muscular body shook and shook as though to shake the life out of itself. The head of the Hyena was thrown back, its throat taut with the passion of its outcry. Then all was over. The fierce head sunk to the level of the huge white-shirted shoulders.

The head of the Hyena turned not to the Boy but to the Goat.

"Do as you're told," he cried. "Insolent dust-bag, clod and filthy knobhead. Do what you're told before I crunch your skull." Hyena turned to the Boy. "He's as dense as a nag's heel. Look at him now."

"Which tree do you mean?" said Goat, scratching himself.

"The nearest tree, Mr. Goat. How is it that you walk? I can't remember. Ah, that's it, that's it! Sideways like a ship in a beam sea. Sideways and edgeways with your cargo slipping. Ah, Mr. Goat, it is strange and haunting, the way you proceed across the face of the earth. Certainly you are a pair of originals, and as such I hail you in the name of Blind Lamb."

"The Blind Lamb," repeated the pair. "Hail to the Blind Lamb."

"And also, in his name," said the Boy, "have mercy on my hunger. That you had thought of your mane as my cradle showed great originality—but I would die of proximity. The working of your muscles would be too much for me. The splendid rankness of your mane would be too strong. The throbbing of your heart would batter me. I have no strength for that. You are so tremendous . . . so majestic. Make me, out of your ingenuity a chair of branches, and carry me both of you . . . carry me . . . where . . . Oh, where will you carry me to?"

"Branches! Branches!" yelled Hyena, taking no notice of the question. "What are you waiting for?" and he gave the Goat a great swipe and then proceeded to break branches off the nearby trees and to thread them together. The tearing of the branches from the main limbs of the trees sounded both loud and terrible in the still air. The Boy sat still, watching these two sinister creatures at work in the shadow of the trees and he wondered how and where he could escape from their vile presence. It was obvious that to escape from them now would lead him to starvation. To whoever it was that they were determined to take him, they would surely have at least bread to eat and water to drink.

The Hyena was on his way back from the trees. He had dropped the saddle-like chair which he had been making and was, it seemed, in a great hurry to reach the Boy. When he arrived he seemed unable to express himself and, although his jaws worked spasmodically, no words ventured forth from his unpleasant mouth. At last in a brutal rush—

"You!" he shouted. "What do you know of the Lamb? The secret Lamb! The Lamb, our Emperor. How dare you talk of the Lamb . . . the Blind Lamb for whom we exist.

We are all that is left of them . . . of all the creatures of the globe; of all insects and all birds—of the fish of the salt ocean and the beasts of prey. For he has changed their natures and they have died. But we did not die. We became as we are through the powers of the Lamb and from his terrible skill. How have you heard of him, you from the white-dust region? Look! You are no more than a youth. How have you heard of him?"

"Oh, I am but a figment of his thought," said the Boy. "I am not really here. Not in my own right. I am here because he made me. But I have wandered—wandered away from his great brain. He does not wish to own me any more. Take me to somewhere where I can eat and drink, then let me go again."

Meanwhile the Goat had reappeared.

"He is hungry," said the Goat, but as he said it the vapid smile on his face froze into something that spelt terror, for from far away there came a sound—a sound that appeared to proceed from unimaginable depths. It was a thin sound, clear as the tinkling of an icicle. Faint, far and clear.

The effect upon the Hyena was as instantaneous as it was upon the Goat. His pointed ears were all at once pricked forward. His head lifted itself high into the air—and the colour of the jowl, which he so carefully shaved each morning, changed from a mottled purple to a deathly pallor.

The Boy, who had heard the call no less than the others, could not imagine why such a sweet and liquid sound should have such an effect upon the two rigid creatures at his side.

"What was that?" he said at last. "Why are you so frightened?"

After a long silence they answered him together.

"That was our Master bleating."

Far away beyond the power of search, in the breathless wastes, where time slides on and on through the sickness of day and the suffocation of the night, there was a land of absolute stillness—a stillness of breath indrawn and held in the lungs—the stillness of apprehension and a dire suspense.

And at the heart of this land or region, where no trees grew,

and no birds sang, there was a desert of grey space that shone
with a metallic light.

Dropping imperceptibly from the four horizons this wide
swathe of terrain, as if drawn in towards a centre, began,
hardly noticeably at first, to break into terraces bright and
lifeless, and, as the level of the surrounding land subsided, the
terraces grew steeper and wider until, just when it appeared
that the focus of this wilderness was at hand, the grey terraces
ceased and there was spread out to the gaze a field of naked
stone. Scattered indiscriminately across this field was what
looked like the chimneys or shafts of old metal workings,
mine-heads, and littered here and there in every direction,
girders and chains. And over it all the light shone horribly on
metal and stone.

And while the mocking sun poured out its beams, and
while there was no other movement in the whole vast amphi-
theatre, there was something stirring, something far below the
level of the ground. Something that was alone and alive,
something that smiled very gently to itself as it sat upon a
throne in a great vaulted chamber, lit by a crowd of candles.

But for all the effulgence thrown out by these candles, the
greater part of the vault was thick with shadow. The contrast
between the dead and glowing light of the outer world with
its hot, metallic sheen, and the chiaroscuro of this subterranean vault, was something that the Goat and the Hyena,
insensitive as they were, never failed to be aware of.

Nor, though the sense of beauty was painfully absent
from their natures, were they ever able to enter this particular
chamber without wonder and stupefaction. Living and sleeping, as they did, in dark and filthy cells, for they were not
allowed so much as a single candle, Hyena and the Goat had
once upon a time been rebellious. They had seen no reason
why, because they were not so intelligent as their overlord,
they should have been worse served in the comforts of life.
But that was very long ago and they had now known for
many years that they were of a lesser breed and that to serve
and obey their master was its own reward. Besides, how would
they survive without his brains? Was it not worth all the
punishment in this subterranean world to be allowed, on rare
occasions, to sit at table with the Emperor and to watch him

drink his wine, and from time to time be allowed a bone to crack?

For all the brutal strength and beastliness of Hyena that rose to the surface whenever he was away from his lord, he became in his presence transmuted into something weak and slavering. And Goat, whose personality was so overpowered by Hyena whenever they met above-ground, was able, under the different conditions, to be quite another creature. The white and fierce grimace which was the Goat's interpretation of a smile was a more or less permanent feature of his long, dusty face. His sidelong walk became almost aggressive, for it was now combined with a kind of swagger; and he swung his arms about more freely under the impression that the more the cuffs were able to be seen the more genteel the wearer.

But this jauntiness was always a thing with a short life, for there lay at the back of everything the sinister presence of their dazzling lord.

White. White as the foam when the moon is full on the sea; white as the white of a child's eye; or the brow of a dead man; white as a sheeted ghost: Oh, white as wool. Bright wool . . . white wool . . . in half a million curls . . . seraphic in its purity and softness . . . the raiment of the Lamb.

And all about it swam the darkness that shifted to the flicker of the candle flames.

For it was a great vault of solemn proportions: a place yawning with silence so that the movement of the little flames was almost like the sound of voices. But there were no animals or insects or birds, or even vegetation to make any noise, nothing at all, except for the lord of the mines, lord of the unworked galleries and of a region deep in the body of the metal. He made no noise. He sat very softly and patiently in a high chair. Immediately before him was a table covered with a cloth of exquisite embroidery. The carpet on which the table was standing was thick and soft and of a very deep blood-red. Here, lost in the nether gloom, the lack of colour in the world above became changed into something that was not merely huelessness but was more than just colour; it was, for reason of the candles and the lamps, a kind of vivid stain; almost as though the lit objects burned—or gave out, rather than absorbed, the light.

But the colours seemed to have no effect upon the Lamb, whose wool reflected nothing but itself and in one other particular, and that was in the matter of the eyes. The pupils were veiled with a dull blue membrane. This blue, dim as it was, had nevertheless a disproportionate effect, for the surrounding features were so angelically white. Set in this exquisite head, the eyes were like two coins.

The Lamb sat very upright, his white hands folded together in his lap. They were exquisite, like the hands of a child, for they were not only tiny, but plump.

It was hard to believe in the primordial ages that lay beneath the down of those white hands. There they were, folded one about the other as though they loved one another; neither gripping one another too passionately, for they were made to be bruised, nor touching one another too lightly, for fear of losing the sweet palpation.

The breast of the lamb was like a little sea—a little sea of curls—of clustered curls or like the soft white crests of moonlight verdure; verdure white as death, frozen to the eye, but voluptuously soft to the touch—and lethal also, for to plunge the hand into that breast would be to find there was no substance there, but only the curls of the lamb—no ribs, no organs; only the yielding, horrible mollience of endless wool.

And there was no heart to be found or to be heard. An ear laid to that deadly breast could hear nothing but a great silence, a wilderness of nothing; an infinite emptiness. And in the silence the two hands separated for a little while and then the finger-tips touched one another in a strangely parsonic way, but only for a moment or two before they fled once again to one another so that their palms rejoined with a sound like a far-away gasp for breath.

This little sound, so infinitesimal in itself, was, nevertheless, in the silence that surrounded the Lamb, quite loud enough to set up a dozen echoes that, making their way into the remotest corners of the deserted galleries, up the throats of prodigious shafts, and, where the great girders and coiling stairs of iron, crossed and re-crossed, split into lesser echoes, so that the whole of this subterranean kingdom became full of inaudible sounds as the air is full of motes.

It was a place forlorn. An emptiness. It was as though a great tide had withdrawn for ever from shores that had once been loud with voices.

There had been a time when these deserted solitudes were alive with hope, excitement and conjecture on how the world was to be changed! But that was far beyond the skyline. All that was left was a kind of shipwreck. A shipwreck of metal. It spiralled; it took great arcs; it rose tier upon tier; it overhung vast wells of darkness; it formed gigantic stairs which came from nowhere and led nowhere. It led on and on; vistas of forgotten metal; moribund, stiff in a thousand attitudes of mortality; with not a rat, not a mouse; not a bat, not a spider. Only the Lamb, sitting in his high chair with a faint smile upon his lips; alone in the luxury of his vaulted chamber, where the red carpet was like blood, and the walls were lined with books that rose up . . . up . . . volume after volume until the shadows engulfed them.

But the Lamb was not happy for, though his brain was clear as ice, yet the hollow where his soul should have been seethed with horrible sickness. For his memory was both sharp and capacious and he could recall not only a time when this adumbrate hall was filled with suppliants of all shapes and kinds at differing stages of mutation and dire change, but the individual characters, ranging as they did, down the centuries each with its idiosyncrasies of gesture, stance and feature; each with its peculiar formations of bone; each with its textures, its mane or its stubble; the spotted, the striped, the skewball or the featureless. He had known them all. He had gathered them in at will, for in those halcyon days the world was alive with creatures, and he had but to call in that sweet voice of his for them to run and cluster at his throne.

But those far, thriving days were dead and gone, for gradually, one by one, they had all died, for the experiments were without precedent. That the Lamb had been able to continue his diabolical pastime, even after his blindness had turned the world into eternal midnight, was proof enough of the quenchless vitality of his evil. No, it was not that the lenses of the eyes had become thick and veiled—it was not anything of that nature that had caused the death of so many—it was that he had *willed* them to become while they were yet men, beasts.

This he could still achieve, for he could feel for and compre-hend the structure of a head and pronounce at once the animal, the prototype that brooded, as it were, behind or within the human shape.

For where the Hyena now advanced with his steep back and his arms and his shaven jaw, and his white shirt, and his hideous laughter, there had once been a man whose tend-ency of feature was towards the beast that now possessed so much of him.

And in the core of the Goat that was now sidling through grey undergrowth, nearer and nearer with every step to the terrible mine-shafts of the underworld, there had once been a man.

For it was the Lamb's exquisite pleasure to debase. To work upon and transform in such a way that through terror and vile flattery subtly intertwined, his unwary victims, one by one, ceased to have a will of their own, but began to dis-integrate not only morally, but palpably. It was then that he exerted a pressure upon them of a hellish kind for, having studied their varying types (the little white fingers fluttering here and there across the bony visages of many a trembling head), he began to will them into a state in which they longed to do what he wished them to do, and be what he wished them to be. So that by degrees the form and character of the beasts they had somewhat resembled began to strengthen and little signs began to appear, such as a note in the voice that had never been there before, or a way of tossing the head like a stag, or lowering it like a hen when it runs to its food.

But the Lamb, so agile of brain, so ingenious, was unable to keep them alive. In most cases this did not matter, but there were some of his beasts who had become, under his terrible aegis, creatures quite superbly idiotic in their propor-tions. Not only so but they, having their curious interplay between the beast and human within them, gave him con-tinued sardonic pleasure, as a dwarf provides diversion for a king. But not for long. The more peculiar were those who died off first, for the whole process of transmutation was of so occult a nature that even the Lamb found it impossible to know what it was that killed them and what it was that kept them alive.

Why it was that somewhere in his complex make-up the Lamb had not only an angry, acrid fire burning, like an ulcer, no one can tell, but it is true that the very sight of a human being caused the colour of his flesh to change. So that it was not only a diversion on his part to drive a human soul into the deep and to find in there its equivalent and counterpart, among the masks of the world, but it was a loathing also—a deep and burning hatred of all humans.

A long time had passed since the last death, when a spider-man cried out for help, curled up, withered before the eyes of the Goat and the Lamb and disintegrated into dust, all in a moment. He had been, for the Lamb, some kind of companion for those rare occasions when the Lamb was in a mood for company. For the Spider had retained the quality of its brain which was an interwoven and tenuous organ, and there were times when, the Lamb sitting on one side of a small ivory table and Spider on the other, they pursued long intellectual battles with some remote affinity to chess.

But this creature had died, and all that was left of the one-time court was the Hyena and the Goat.

Nothing seemed to kill these two. They lived on and on. The Lamb would sometimes sit and stare in their direction and, although it could see nothing, it could hear everything. So keen was its sense of hearing and of smell that, although the two creatures and the Boy were still long leagues away, yet they could even now be heard and smelt distinctly by this white overlord as he sat very upright with his hands folded.

But what was that faint and unfamiliar scent that came floating to the mines along with the more pungent odours of the Hyena and the Goat? At first there was no change in the position of the Lamb but then, although the white head tilted back, the rest of the body remained immobile. The milk-white ears were pricked forward, and the sensitive nostrils quivered with the speed of an adder's tongue or of a bee's wing when it hovers above a flower. The eyes gazed blindly into the darkness overhead. All about him in the darkest areas or where the lamplight gloated on the terraced spines of his library, something quite different was at large; a sense of quickening. The inscrutable Lamb, who had never been known to show his feelings, had parted, for a moment, with his own nature, for not only had he withdrawn as it were his head upon his shoulders, thus accentuating the rigidity of his posture, but an all-but-invisible tremor passed over his blind face.

For the smell of life approaching grew keener every moment, though the distance between the subterranean mines and the stumbling trio was still a matter of many miles.

The three of them, led by the Hyena, had by now covered quite a tract of country. They had left the motionless woods behind them and had reached a belt of desiccated shrubs through which they waded. By now the heat had gone out of the day and the Boy's hunger was causing him to cry.

"What are his eyes doing, my dear?" said the Goat, pointing as he did so with what looked like a handless arm, for the long semi-starched and dirty cuffs reached far beyond the hands and fingers.

"Stop for a moment, Hyena, love. What he is doing reminds me of something."

"Oh, it does, does it, you son of a green stench? And what would that be? Eh?"

"Look and see for yourself, with your beautiful, clever face," said the Goat. "Can you see what I mean? Turn your head to me, Boy, so that your betters can enjoy the full of your countenance. You see, Hyena, dear, is it not as I told you? His eyes are full of bits of broken glass. Feel them, Hyena, feel them! They are wet and warm, and look—both his cheeks are swimming with water. It reminds me of something. What is it . . . ?"

"How should I know?" barked Hyena, irritably.

"Look," continued the Goat. "I can stroke his eyelids. How the white lord will love to readjust him!"

A vague, unformulated fear swept through the Boy though he could not understand what the Goat meant by 'readjustment.' Without knowing quite what he was doing, he struck out at the Goat, but in his weakness and tiredness the blow was so feeble that, although it landed on the shoulder of the Goat, yet the creature felt nothing, but went on talking.

"Hyena, dear!"

"What you hornhead?"

"Can you remember far enough . . ."

"Far enough *what?*" growled the Hyena, his smooth jaws working like clockwork.

"Far enough *back*, my love," whispered the Goat, scratching himself, so that the dust poured out of his hide like smoke escaping from a chimney. "Far enough back," he repeated.

The Hyena shook his mane irritably. "Far enough back for *what*—you knobhead?"

"For those long seasons, those decades, dear, those centuries. Don't you remember . . . before we were changed . . . when our limbs were beastless. We were, you know, my sweet Hyena, we *were* once."

"We were *what*? Speak up, you damned Goat, or I'll crack you like a rib."

"We were different once. You had no mane on your sloping back. It is very beautiful, but it wasn't there. And your long forearms."

"What about them?"

"Well, they weren't always brindled, were they, dear?"

Hyena spat a cloud of bone-powder from between his powerful teeth. Then he leapt without warning at his colleague.

"Silence," he cried, in a voice that at any moment might have veered into that terrible mournful cry which in turn might have let loose the diabolical laughter of the insane.

Standing with one of its feet planted upon the Goat, for Hyena had banged him to the ground, "Silence," he cried again. "I do not want to remember."

"Nor do I," said the Goat. "But I can remember *little* things. Curious *little* things. Before we changed, you know."

"I said, silence!" said the Hyena, but this time there was something almost ruminative in the tone of his voice.

"You are bruising my ribs," said Goat. "Have pity, my dear. You are too savage with your friends. Ah . . . thank you, love. Bless me, you have a splendid—look at the Boy."

"Bring him back," said Hyena, "and I'll skin him."

"He is for our white lord," said the Goat. "I will cuff him."

The Boy had indeed wandered away, but only for a few yards. At the touch of the Goat he sank to his knees as though he had been felled like a young tree.

"I can remember quite a lot," said the Goat, returning to Hyena. "I can remember when my brow was clear and smooth."

"Who cares?" yelled Hyena, in a fresh surge of temper. "Who cares about your bloody brow?"

"And I can tell you something else," said the Goat.

"What's that?"

"About this Boy."

"What about him?"

"He must not die before the White Lord sees him. Look at him, Hyena. No! No! Hyena, dear. Kicking him will not help. Perhaps he is dying. Pick him up, Hyena. You are the noble one; you are the powerful one. Pick him up and gallop to the mines. To the mines, my dear, while I race on ahead."

"What for?"

"To have his supper ready. He must have bread and water, mustn't he?"

The Hyena darted a mean and sidelong glance at the Goat before it turned to the Boy on the ground, and then, hardly stooping, caught him up in his brindled arms as though there were no weight at all.

So they set off again, the Goat trying to forge ahead, but he had not reckoned with the long, loping, sinewy run of his rival, whose voluminous white shirt billowed out behind. Sometimes it seemed that one of them was flagging, and sometimes another—but for the most part they ran abreast.

The Boy was too far gone with exhaustion to understand what was happening. He did not even know that he was being held out at full length by Hyena rather as though he were a sacrifice. One advantage of this was that the odour of the powerful half-beast was to some extent mitigated, although it is doubtful whether the Boy's state of collapse allowed his amelioration to be appreciated.

Mile after mile they ran. The sea of shrubs through which they had waded for the last several miles had now given place to a thick kind of silvery rock-face, over which the Goat and the Hyena ran as though they were part of some immemorial legend, their long, drawn-out shadows bounding beside them, while the sun slid down the sky in a blur of hue-less light. And then, suddenly, as the dark thickened, they felt the first sign that the ground was dropping away and that they had come to the great terraces that led downwards to the Mines. And sure enough, there it was, that widespread congregation of ancient and deserted chimneys, their edges glinting in the early moonlight.

On seeing the chimneys Hyena and Goat came to a halt. Why they did so is not hard to guess, for they were now as much in the presence of the Lamb as they would be standing before him. From now on every single sound, no matter how faint, would be loud in the ears of their Master.

They both knew this by bitter experience, for in the far-off days they had, along with other half-men, made the mistake of whispering to one another, not realizing that the merest breath was sucked into the great flues and chimneys and so down to the central areas where they turned and twisted, threading their way to where the Lamb sat upright, his ears and nostrils pricking with sentience.

Masters in the art of deaf and dumb language and also of lip-reading, they chose the latter, for the dangling position of the Goat's white cuffs obscured the fingers. So, staring one another in the face, they mouthed their words in deathly silence.

"He knows . . . we . . . are . . . here . . . Hyena . . . dear."

"He . . . can . . . smell . . . us . . . by . . . now. . . ."

"And . . . the . . . Boy. . . ."

"Of . . . course . . . of . . . course. . . . My . . . stomach's . . . turning . . . over. . . ."

"I . . . will . . . go . . . first . . . with . . . the . . . Boy . . . and . . . prepare . . . his . . . supper . . . and . . . his . . . bed."

"You . . . will . . . not . . . you . . . hornhead . . . Leave . . . him . . . to . . . me . . . or . . . I . . . will . . . crush . . . you."

"Then . . . I . . . will . . . go . . . alone. . . ."

"Of . . . course . . . you . . . dust . . . trap. . . ."

"He . . . must . . . be . . . washed . . . to-night, and . . . fed . . . and . . . given . . . water. That is . . . for you . . . to do . . . since . . . you . . . insist. I . . . will . . . acquaint

our Master . . . Oh . . . my green . . . loins. . . . My . . .
loins. . . . My terrified . . . loins. . . ."

They turned and withdrew from one another, their lips
ceased to move, but as they ended their conversation they
brought their lips together and in his sanctum the White
Lamb heard the sound of the cessation, a sound resembling
that of a cobweb crumbling to the floor or the step of a mouse
on moss.

So the Hyena went on alone, carrying the Boy before him
in his hands, until he came to the foot of a prodigious shaft
more like an abyss than anything consciously constructed.
And here, on the edge of this great well of darkness, he knelt
down and, clasping his horrid hands together, he whispered:

"White Lord of Midnight, Hail!"

The five words fell almost palpably down the throat of the
herbless, lifeless shaft and, echoing their way netherwards,
came at last into the orbit of the Lamb's reception.

"It is Hyena, my lord, Hyena, whom you rescued from the
upper void. Hyena, who came to you, to love you and serve
your purposes. Hail!"

Then came a voice from the abysmal darkness. It was like
a little bell tinkling, or the sound of naked innocence, or the
crowing of a babe . . . or the bleating of a Lamb.

"You have somebody with you, I believe?"

The little voice trilled out of the darkness; it had no need
to be raised. Like a needle piercing its way through rotten
fabric, so this sweet sound penetrated to the furthermost re-
cesses of the Underground Kingdom. It reached, trill upon
echoing trill, into the dungeons away to the west, where,
among the twisted girders of red rust, the silent floors were
noduled with a sea of purple mushrooms, dead as the ground
they had once risen from. It needed but the stamp of a foot
to bring them down in a great death of colourless dust—
no foot, no gust of air, nothing had passed that way for a
hundred years.

It penetrated in every direction, this voice of the Lamb's . . .
and now it spoke again.

"I am waiting for your answer . . . and for you."

Then, with a thin sigh like the sound of a scythe, "What

have you brought back for me from out of the vile sunlight? What have you got for your lord? I am still waiting."

"We have a Boy."

"A Boy?"

"A Boy—touchless."

There was a long silence during which Hyena thought he could hear something which he had never heard before, a remote throbbing.

But the voice of the Lamb was as clear and sweet and fresh as a water-shoot and quite emotionless.

"Where is the Goat?"

"The Goat," said Hyena, "has done everything to hinder me. Shall I come down, my lord?"

"I think that what I said was 'Where is the Goat?' I am not interested in whether or not he hinders you or you hinder him. What interests me at the moment is his whereabouts. Wait! Do I hear him in the Southern Gallery?"

"Yes, Master," said the Hyena. He thrust his head and shoulders so far over the edge of the abyss that it would seem dangerous to anyone unacquainted with his miraculous head for heights and his general agility in dark and precipitous places.

"Yes, Master. The Goat is descending by the iron staircase. He has gone to prepare the Boy his bread and water. The hairless thing has fainted. You would not wish to see him, my White Lord, until he has been washed, fed and rested. Nor do you want to see the Goat, that stupid crackhead. I will not allow him to irk you."

"You are strangely kind to-day," came the sweet voice from the depths. "So I am sure you will do what I tell you; for if you do otherwise I shall have your black mane burned away. So come at once with your exhausted friend and I will size him up. I can smell him already and I must say he is like a breath of fresh air in the place. Are you on your way? I don't hear anything." The Lamb had bared its pearly teeth.

"I am on my way . . . Master . . . on my way . . ." cried the Hyena, who was shaking with fear, for the Lamb's voice was like a knife in a velvet sheath. "I will bring him to you now to be yours for ever," and Hyena, his legs and arms still trembling in spite of all their strength, began to lower himself and the Boy over the edge of the pit, where a chain shone dimly in the moonlight.

In order to have both hands free for swarming down the iron chain, Hyena had slung the Boy over his shoulder, where he moaned pitifully.

But Hyena cared nothing about this, for he had recognized a note of a different blend in the Lamb's voice. He still spoke as gently, as horribly gently as before, but there was a difference now. What it was exactly that gave Hyena the impression that the voice had altered it is impossible to say, for Hyena could only *feel* the change, and the feel of it was that of hidden fervour.

Indeed what cause there was! Any creature of lesser calibre than the Lamb would by now have been unable to control the horrid thrill of his excitement.

For a decade or more had passed since the last visitor sat down at table with him—sat down and saw the veiled eyes of the Lamb, and knew even as he stared at his host that his soul was being sucked out of him. He had died, like the rest, the brain running away too sharply from the body or the body leaping like a frog in search of the brain, so that they broke apart, and, like the machinery of the Mines, they died away into silence and emptiness of death.

What it was that kept the last two underlings alive even the Lamb did not know. Something in their natures or in their organs gave the Goat and the Hyena some sort of physical immunity—something, perhaps, to do with their general coarseness of soul and fibre. They had outlived a hundred powerful beasts whose metamorphoses had in time destroyed them from within. The Lion, only an age ago, had collapsed in a mockery of power, bending his great head as he did so, the tears welling from the amber eyes, to thread their way down tracts of golden cheek-bone. It was a great and terrible fall: yet it was merciful, for, under the macabre aegis of the dazzling Lamb, the one-time king of beasts was brought to degradation, and there is nothing more foul than the draining of the heart's blood, drop by drop, from the great golden cat.

Collapsing with a roar, it had, so it seemed, dragged down the night, as though it were a curtain, and when the lanterns had been lit again there was nothing there, but a cloak and breastplate and a dagger bright with stars, and floating away into the unutterable darkness of the western vaults, the mane of the great half-beast, like an aura.

And there had been the Man, delicate and nimble, across whose face the Lamb had drawn his finger, so that he knew, in his blindness, by touch and a quivering in the air that he was pure gazelle. But he had died a century after, at the exquisite height of a bound, his great eyes losing lustre as he fell—

And there had been the mantis man, the pig man and the dogs: the crocodile, the raven and that inordinate fish that sang like a linnet. But they had all died at one stage or another in their transmutation for lack of some ingredient, some necessity for survival, which for some obscure reason Hyena and the Goat possessed.

It was a source of chagrin to the Lamb that of all the divers creatures to have passed through his tiny, snow-white hands, creatures of all shapes, sizes and intellects, he should find himself left at last with a couple of near-idiots—the cowardly and bullying Hyena and the sycophantic Goat. There was a time when his secret vault with its rich carpets, golden candlesticks; incense burning in beakers of jade and its crimson awnings swaying a little from the distant up-draught of the air-shafts—there was a time when this sanctum had been filled with his heirophants who, awestruck at the sight of such a place, peered over one another's shoulders (shoulders of fur, shoulders of bristle, shoulders of raw hide, shoulders of scale and feather) at their lord, while he, the Lamb, the creator as it were of a new kingdom, a new species, sat on his highbacked throne, the dull blue membrane covering his eyes, his breast sumptuous with soft and peerless curls, his hands folded, his faintly tinctured lips the most delicate of mauves, and on his head, on rare occasions, a crown of delicate bones exquisitely interwoven, bleached to a whiteness that rivalled the very wool that was his raiment.

This crown was constructed from the thin bones of a stoat and indeed it seemed that something of the stoat's mercurial and terrible vitality had remained in the marrow of the filigree structure, for when the Lamb, out of the diabolical hell of its heart, discovered his own heinous power to hold a victim rooted to the ground so that the blood within the creature yearned for annihilation at the hands of the torturer, the heart pounding against its will, then was it like the swaying stoat with its upright carriage and its kiss of death upon the jugular.

And indeed the Goat had seen it in the Lamb: and the Hyena also. That mesmeric swaying, that upright back. All but the kiss of death. All but the jugular. For the White Lamb was not interested in corpses (though they filled the darkness with their bones), but only in playthings.

And all he had left was the Hyena and the Goat. Yet he still held court. He was still the Lord of the Mines, though it was a great length of time since he had worn the Crown, for he had given up hope of new victims.

Year after year, decade after decade, in this subterranean world of silence and of death nothing had stirred, nothing had moved, not even the dust; nothing but their voices from time to time, when the Goat or Hyena reported at close of day, recounting to the Lamb the tale of each day's search. Search: fruitless search! That was the burden of their lives. That was their purpose. To find another human, for the Lamb itched for his talents to burgeon once again. For he was like a pianist manacled, the keyboard before him. Or a famished gourmet unable to reach, but able to see a table spread with delicacies.

But all this was over and the Lamb, though he made no sign, and though his voice was as smooth and even as oil on water, was consumed with an exquisite apprehension, quite terrible in its intensity.

The Lamb could hear two voices, one of them proceeding from the gigantic funnel to the north and the other, a good mile further to the east, much fainter but perfectly clear . . . a kind of obsequious shuffling.

The other noise was altogether more imminent, and was of course proceeding from the nearby shaft where Hyena lowered himself link by link through the darkness with the Boy slung over his hirsute shoulders. As he descended three sounds preceded him: the grinding and straining of the iron links, a slow panting in the beast's capacious chest, and the munching of small bones.

The Lamb, in his sanctum, alone, save for the loudening sound of his henchmen, sat very upright. Although his eyes were veiled and sightless, yet his entire face had something about it that was watchful. The head was not cocked upon one side: the ears were not pricked: there was no quivering to be seen: no tension: yet never was a creature as alert, as vile, as predatory. Cold horror was returning to the sanctum: the throbbing horror of the will. For the scent in the nostrils of the Lamb had by now become more specific. The field of odour had narrowed and it was now no longer a matter of conjecture as to what it was that the Lamb would soon be touching with his soft white hand. He would be touching nothing less than flesh entirely *human*.

He could not, as yet, determine such niceties as the age of the captive, for he was shrouded in the fumes of iron that spread from the long chain, and the smell of the earth through which the well-head had been bored, not to speak of the indescribable effluvia of the Hyena—and a hundred other emanations.

But with every yard of descent these varying odours detached themselves one from another and there came the moment when, with absolute surety, Lamb knew that there was a Boy in the shaft.

A Boy in the shaft. A Boy from the Other Region . . . approaching . . . descending. . . . This in itself was enough to cause the very girders of the Mines to coil and spill red rust-like sand. It was enough to start exciting echoes— echoes unparented. Echoes that cried like demons: echoes at large like ears among the shadows: echoes of consternation: echoes delirious: echoes barbaric: echoes of exultation.

For the world had forsaken the Mines, and time had forgotten them: yet here was the world again: the globe in microcosm. A human . . . a Boy . . . something to break . . . or to batter down, as though it were clay . . . and then to build again.

Meanwhile, as the moments passed, and the Hyena and the Boy drew nearer and nearer to the sumptuous vault below them where the Lamb sat immobile as a marble carving save only for the flickering of his dilated nostrils—the Goat, away to the west, had reached the wide and empty floor of the Mines, and was shuffling along in that horrible sideways gait of his, the left shoulder always in advance of the rest of his body. And as he made his furtive way he muttered to himself, for he was full of grievance. What right had Hyena to have all the credit? Why should Hyena make the presentation? It had been he, the Goat, who had found the human. It was bitterly unfair: a hotness of anger burned like a live coal beneath his ribs. The cuffs of his jacket shook and his tombstone teeth were displayed in what could be taken either for a grin or a threat.

In fact it was a sign of frustration and hatred, a rankling hatred, for this was a moment never again to be repeated, a moment of such dramatic importance to the three of them that there should have been no question of rivalry for favour.

Could they not have approached their Emperor, the Lamb, together? Could they not have held the prisoner, one on either side, and made their bow together, and offered him together? Oh, it was most unjust, and the Goat beat his hands together at his sides, and a nasty sweat poured down his long face, on the damp bristles through which his yellow eyes shone pale coins.

So strongly did he feel all this that he now began unconsciously to think of the Boy almost as a brother in distress: someone who, because of his hatred for Hyena (and this had been obvious from the first moment), had become, automatically, and by pure retaliation, an ally.

But there was nothing he could do, in his pent-up condition, save make his way towards the Vault some short way from which in his own dank quarters he would (as a gesture, or a slap in Hyena's face), he would prepare his own bed for the Boy and stave his hunger and thirst with water and sour bread.

It was obvious that the Boy's need for sleep and sustenance outweighed any other factor, for what possible advantage could there be to the Lamb to see the thing he had been waiting for, for so many years, in a state of collapse?

He would wish for an alert and sentient prey, and it was the Goat's plan to put this point to the Lamb himself.

It was therefore a matter of great moment that the Goat should make all speed to the sumptuous sanctum of the Lamb, and he began to run as he had never run before.

On every side of him, above him, and sometimes below

him the derelict remains of iron structures spread out their wild and subterranean arms. Brandished in giant loops: coiling in twisted stairways that led to nowhere, these relics of another age unfurled their iron fantasies as Goat sped by, covering the ground with quite unnatural pace.

It was very dark, but he knew this track of old and never by so much as a touch did he disturb a fragment of the litter that lay scattered on the wide floor. He knew it as an Indian knows the secret track through the woods and, like the Indian, he was ignorant of the great fastness that lay on either side.

There came the time when the ground descended in a slow slope and the Goat, still running edgeways-on as though all hell was after him, came to the outskirts of that central dereliction where in his vault the White Lamb sat and waited.

Even the formidable muscles of Hyena were tested by such a climb, but he was now no more than a dozen feet from the subterranean floor, where every sound was amplified and echoes shuffled from wall to wall.

The Boy was no longer in a faint: his head had cleared but his hunger was keener than ever and his limbs felt like water.

Once or twice he had raised himself a little from the shoulders of the half-beast but had fallen back again for lack of strength, although the mane upon which he fell was, for all the oiling that Hyena gave it, as coarse and thick as tare-grass.

Directly he landed he turned from the swinging chain and fixed his eyes upon the outer wall of the Vault. Had he gazed up the throat of the ancient mine-shaft he would have seen, for his eyes were as keen as an eagle's, a pin-prick in the darkness; the colour of blood. It was all that could be seen of the sunset, that grain of crimson. But Hyena was not interested in staring up at crimson pin-heads, but in the fact that he was now within a hundred feet of the Lamb.

He knew that even his breathing was overheard by his inscrutable lord, and he was about to take his first step forward when there was a sudden trampling to his left and a dusty creature in a black coat slewed itself into the picture and only drew up when it was within a yard of its irritable colleague. For it was of course the Goat, the dusty-headed Goat who had, to Hyena's amazement, a grin upon his face,

a real grin and no mere show of teeth. It was not long before
he knew the reason, and had it not been that every sound
that was made was loud in the Lamb's ear, there is no doubt
the Goat would have been savaged mercilessly, if not killed
by the merciless Hyena.

For, during the last part of the Goat's solitary flight through
the galleries and girders an idea had come to him, born of
his hatred for Hyena who had so callously stolen from him
the golden chance of pleasing the Lamb.

Hyena, though unaware of the meaning of the Goat's grin,
yet knew no good could come of its implications, whatever
they were, and he shook with suppressed rage as he glared
murderously at his mulcted foe.

Unshouldering himself of the Boy, who slid to the ground,
the Hyena, using the language of the deaf and dumb—for the
faintest whisper would have sounded to the Lamb like the
cracking and hissing of a forest fire—made rapid signs to
the Goat which told that he proposed at the earliest opportunity to hack him to death.

In return the Goat, who mouthed his words syllable by
syllable with his purplish lips, advised his enemy with a horrid
oath to do no such thing, and then, to Hyena's amazement,
turned away and, facing the outer walls of the sanctum, lifted
his mealy voice.

"Lord Emperor and ever-dazzling Lamb," he said.

"O thou by whom we live and breathe and are! Sun of our
nether darkness, listen to your slave. For I have found him!"

There was a sudden wrenching sound, as of strangulation,
as the Hyena, lifting his long, mean head, strained, as it were,
on an invisible leash. His blood had mounted into his head
and his eyes shone with a red light.

There was no sound from the Lamb so the Goat continued.

"I found him for you on the dusty plains. There I subdued
him, brought him to his knees, drew from his belt his dagger:
threw it away to where it sank in dust as a stone sinks in
water; trussed him, and brought him to the minehead. There,
lounging in the sun, I found Hyena. The muscular Hyena,
the foul Hyena—"

"Lies! Lies! ! You slavering knobhead."

"All lies! my lord. He never even—"

There came out of the gloom a gentle bleating—a sound sweet as April.

"Be quiet, children. Where is this human youth?"

As Hyena was about to tell the Lamb that the Boy was lying at his feet, the Goat whipped in with his answer—

"We have him, sir, prone on the earth floor. I suggest that he is fed, given water and then allowed to sleep. I shall prepare my bed for him, if you agree. Hyena's couch is foul with filthy bristles and hairs from his striped arms, and white with powder from the bones he munches. He could not sleep in such a place as that. Nor has Hyena any bread to give him. He is so bestial, my ivory lord: so unspeakably vile."

But the Goat had gone too far and found himself at once upon his back. Over him loomed the trembling febrile and muscular darkness of Hyena. His jaws opening to their fullest disclosed a crimson world walled in with teeth—which, as they were about to close with a crack like gunfire, were held quivering in mid-air by that flute-like voice again, for the Lamb was calling. . . .

"Bring me the youth that I may touch his temple. Is he unconscious?"

The Hyena knelt down upon his knees and stared at the Boy. Then he nodded his head. He had not recovered from the fabrications of the Goat nor from the uprush of anger he had just sustained.

The Boy, who was wide awake, felt a kind of extra sickness, and knew intuitively that above all he must pretend at this moment to be unconscious or to be dead, and as the Goat bent over to inspect him, he held his breath for twenty long seconds. The proximity of the Goat was frightful to endure; but at last the creature rose and called out softly in the gloom:

"Insensible, O Lamb. Insensible as my horny hoof."

"Then bring him to me, my pretty wranglers, and forget your puny rage. It is not you or the sound of you that interests me, but the human youth. I am very old and so can sense the youth of him against me: and I am very young, so I can sense his nearness to my soul. Bring him to me now, before you wash him, dress him and give him food and sleep. Bring him to me, for my finger itches—"

And then suddenly there came from the throat of the Lamb

a cry so shrill that had the Hyena or the Goat been looking at the Boy they could not have failed to see him start where he lay as though someone had pierced him with a needle. It was a cry so excruciatingly shrill and so unexpected that the Goat and Hyena drew closer together for all their hatred of one another. They had never, down the long decades, ever heard their lord throw out such a sound. It was as though, in spite of his grasp upon himself, the Lamb was yet unable to control the emotional pressure that filled his milk-white body—and so this jet of sound sprang through the darkness.

It was a long while before the high-pitched echoes died away and the yawning silence returned.

But it was not only that the sound had been shrill and sudden: there had been something else about it. It was no mere matter of the lungs or the vocal chords. It sprang from the uttermost pit of evil—a spearhead, a lance, a forerunner of dire menace. All that the Lamb had hidden for long centuries had shrilled its way through darkness into light.

But the Lamb was outwardly the same and sat if anything more upright than ever, the only difference being that the little snow-white hands were no longer folded. They were raised to the height of the shoulders in a gesture almost of a supplicant or of a mother holding an invisible child. The index fingers, curving a little inward, suggested, however, some kind of beckoning.

The head was bent back a little on the shoulders and looked as though it might strike forward at any moment like a cobra. The veiled eyes in their dull blue opacity appeared almost to see through the membrane. The Hyena and the Goat came forward supporting the Boy by his elbows.

Step by step they drew nearer to the Lamb, until they came to the wall that surrounded the innermost sanctum and when they were only a few feet from the heavy curtains that formed the entrance they heard a sound of bleating, so faint, so far away; it was like innocence or a strain of love from the pastures of sweet April.

That was a sound they knew (the Goat and the Hyena) and they shuddered, for it brought with it no more love than can be found in a vampire's tongue.

"Once I have run my finger down his brow"—came the

soft voice, "and slid it down the profile to the chin, then take him from me, feed him and sleep him. I can smell his fatigue. If either or both of you should lose him in the Mines" —continued the Voice as sweet as honey and as light as bird-song—"I will make you eat each other."

Under his mane the Hyena turned as white as the bones he gnawed and the Goat heaved with a sudden abortive sickness. "Come in, my dears, and bring your treasure with you."

"I come, master," cried the gruff voice of Hyena—"I come, O, my Emperor!"

"I have found him for you," echoed the Goat, not to be outdone; and as they pushed their way through the curtains the Boy, unable to resist the temptation, opened his eyelids the merest fraction and stared through his eyelashes. It was only for a moment, and his eyes closed again but he had seen in that short space of time that the abode of the white Lamb was lit by many candles.

"Why do you keep me waiting, gentlemen?" The unnaturally sweet accents floated from above, for the chair in which the Lamb sat was a tall, sculpted affair, a good deal higher than is usual. "Must I tell you to lie upon your backs and suffer?

"Now then . . . now then, where is he . . . ? Bring me the mortal."

It was then that the Boy went through his darkest hell of all: the long ache of his body, acute as it was, was yet forgotten or disposed of in some way, for he was filled with a disembodied pain, an illness so penetrating, so horrible, that had he been given the opportunity to die he would have taken it. No normal sensation could find a way through this overpowering nausea of the soul that filled him.

For he was getting nearer and nearer to an icy aura that hung about the face of the Lamb. An aura like death, gelid and ghastly—yet febrile also and terrible in its vitality—yet all was contained and held between the outlines of the long inscrutable visage, for, even when the Lamb had screamed, the face remained immobile, as though the head and the voice were strangers to one another.

This long face with its vibrance and its icy emanations was now very close to the Boy, who did not dare to raise his eyes, though he knew the Lamb was sightless. Then came the moment when the little finger of the Lamb's left hand moved forward like a short, white caterpillar and, hovering for a little while near the victim's forehead, finally descended, and the Boy felt a touch on his brow that brought his heart into his throat.

For the finger of the Lamb appeared to suck at the temple like the sucker of an octopus, and then as the digit traced the profile it left behind it from the hair-line to the chin a track or wake so cold that his brow contracted with pain.

And that was enough, that tracing, to teach the Lamb all that he wished to know. In one sweep of the finger he had discovered that he had in the darkness before him a thing of quality, a thing of youth and style; something of pride, of a mortal unbeasted.

The effect upon the innermost system of the Lamb must have been horrible indeed for, although there appeared to be no visible excitement in the way he got to his feet and raised his blind face to the darkness overhead, yet at that moment when he moved his finger from the Boy's chin, a kind of covetous and fiery rash spread out beneath the wool, so that the milk-white curls appeared to be curdled, in a blush from head to feet.

"Take him away at once," he whispered, "and when this coma leaves him, and when he is fed and strong again, return him to me. For he is what your white lord has awaited. His very bones cry out for realignment: his flesh to be reshaped; his heart to be shrivelled, and his soul to feed on fear."

The Lamb was still standing. He raised his arms on either side like an oracle. His hands fluttered at the extremities of his arms like little white doves.

"Take him away. Prepare a feast. Forget nothing. My crown: the golden cutlery. The poison bottles; and the fumes; the wreaths of ivy and the bloody joints; the chains; the bowl of nettles; the spices; the baskets of fresh grass; the skulls and spines; the ribs and shoulder-blades. Forget nothing or, by the blindness of my sockets, I will have your hearts out.

"Take him away. . . ."

Without waiting a moment Hyena and the Goat backed

clumsily out of the candle-lit vault and the heavy curtains fell back heavily into place.

As usual after a session with their ghastly lord, the two half-beasts clung together for a little while after the swinging back of the curtains, and the presence of their dank bodies was almost more than the Boy could stand, for he was wedged between them. Their internecine feud was by now forgotten in the fearful excitement: for they were to be witnesses of transformation. Together they put the Boy to bed (if a mouldering couch can be called a bed) and they fed him from an old tin of mashed-up bread and water. There was something almost lovable in the way they watched him lift his head to the wooden spoon. Their concentration was so childlike.

For a moment before the Boy fell asleep he gazed up at the two strange nurses and there flashed through his mind the thought that, if need be, he could outwit them both.

Then he turned over and collapsed into a thick and dreamless sleep while the Goat, sitting beside him, scratched interminably at his dusty head, while the Hyena, an ulna between his jaws, munched away in the darkness.

After about five hours of watching over the sleep-drugged Boy the two sentries got to their feet and made their way to the candle-lit Vault. There being no reply to Hyena's query as to whether or not they might enter, they drew the curtains softly aside and peered in. At first they could see nothing. The spines of the books that filled one of the walls gleamed in the gloating light. The sumptuous red carpet flooded the floor: but the high chair was empty. Where was the Lamb?

Then they saw him, all at once, and with a start of recognition. His back was towards them and such was the vagary of the light that standing there he was beyond the range of two clusters of candles, he was all but invisible. But a little time later he moved a little to the west and they saw his hands.

And yet, at the same time, they did not see his hands, for they were moving so fast one about another, circling one another, separating, threading and weaving their ten fantastic fingers in such a delirium of movement, that nothing could be seen but an opalescent blurr of light that sometimes rose, sometimes sank and sometimes hovered like a mist at the

height of the White Lamb's breast. What was happening?
What was he doing? The Hyena shot a sideways glance at
his companion and found no enlightenment there. How could
they know that such were the fermentations in the brain of
the Lamb that they could not be endured a moment longer
without the aid of the body; for there comes a time when the
brain, flashing through constellations of conjecture, is in
danger of losing itself in worlds from which there is no return.
And so the body, in its wisdom, flies alongside, ready, by
means of its own rapidity, to grapple, if the need arose, with
the dazzling convolutions of the brain. What the Hyena and
the Goat were witnessing was just this. The intellectual
excitement which the Boy aroused in the Lamb was of just
such an order, so that as it mounted in intensity, the little
white fingers, rising intuitively to the occasion, held, by means
of their own agility and speed, madness at bay.

All this was lost upon the two watchers through the curtain, but this was not to say that they were too dense to
realize that this was not the right moment for disturbing their
master. What it was that he was doing they did not know,
but they knew enough to realize that it was something out
of their own crass realm. So they retired as silently as possible,
and made their way to the midnight kitchens and the
armoury, and the baskets of fresh grass and all else that per-
tained to the Feast—and began, though they had many hours
in hand, to polish the gold plate, the Crown, and the shoulder-
blades.

By now the Lamb, having subdued the speed of his own
thought, had brought his hands together, as though in prayer
and was now draped in a black shawl.

The Boy slept on . . . and on . . . and the hours moved
slowly by, and the silence of the great subterranean mines
became like a noise in itself—a kind of droning as of bees in
a hollow tree; but eventually while Goat and Hyena, resting
at last from their labours, sat and stared at the sleeping mortal,
the Boy awoke, and as he awoke he heard the Hyena rouse
itself and spit out of its mouth a cloud of white bone-dust.
Turning his head, the Hyena scowled at his confederate and
then, for no apparent reason, he reached out a long, brindled
arm and brought it down heavily on the Goat's head.

This thump, that might have killed a man, merely shook the Goat badly and to ward off the possibilities of the Hyena repeating the attack the Goat showed his teeth in a grin both ingratiating and beastly; though it was true this smile was to some extent shrouded by the cloud of rising dust that billowed up from the Goat's head.

The Boy half-opened his eyes and saw the Hyena immediately above him.

"Why did you strike me, Hyena, dear?" said the Goat.

"Because I wanted to."

"Ah. . . ."

"I loathe your loose purple lips—"

"Ah. . . ."

"And your hairy belly—"

"I am sorry they displease you, dear."

"Listen!"

"Yes, my love."

"What will the White Lamb make of him, I wonder? Eh, you knobhead? What will he be? Eh?"

"O Hyena dear, shall I *tell* you what *I* think? . . ."

"What?"

"A Hare!"

"No! No! No!"

"Why not, dear?"

"Silence, you fool! A cockerel!"

"Oh, no, dear."

"What do you dare to mean? I said a cockerel!"

"Or a rabbit?"

"No! No! No!"

"Or a porpoise? His skin is so smooth."

"So was yours before the bristles rose. He'll build a burning cockerel from his bones."

"Our Lord the Lamb will know."

"Our Lord will bestialize him."

"Then there'll be three of us."

"Four, you fool! Four!"

"But the Lamb?"

"He is not one of us. He is . . ."

"He *is not one of us*. . . ."

Whose voice was that? Whose was it? It was not theirs and it was not the Lamb's!

The two half-beasts leapt to their feet and stared about them until their gaze fell upon the Boy. His eyes were wide open, and it seemed in the semi-darkness that they were as alert and watchful as the eyes of a tracker. Not a muscle of his face moved, but his stomach swam with fearful apprehension.

From the very first when he had been accosted by the Goat he had, bit by bit, been able to piece together a foul, fantastic and unholy picture. A peculiar horror seeped through the heinous place, but this he now knew to be mere background to a nameless crime. The scattered sentences; the word here, the ejaculation there, had made it all too clear that he was to be sacrificed.

There was, nevertheless, a chip of granite at the heart of the Boy. Something obdurate. There was also something in his head. It was a brain.

It is hard for a brain to work adroitly when the hands are swimming in sweat and the stomach is retching with fear and nausea. But with a concentration quite fierce in its intensity he repeated yet again, *"He is not one of us."*

The lips of the Hyena had drawn themselves back from the powerful teeth with a bewildered snarl. The powerful body appeared to vibrate beneath the voluminous white shirt. The hands gripped one another as though they fought in deadly grapple.

As for the Goat, it sidled alongside its colleague and peered at the boy with eyes the colour of lemon peel.

"One of us? The idea is absurd, gentlemen. We know better than to trust that baa-lamb."

The Boy crept nearer to the pair, his finger to his lips until, when he was almost touching them, he began to mouth his words in absolute silence.

"I have great news for you," he said. "Watch my mouth closely.

"You shall be Kings then indeed! For you are characters, gentlemen: characters in your own right. You have brains; you have muscles; you have resource; and, what is more important, you have the will to accomplish. . . ."

"The will to accomplish what?" said the Hyena, spitting out a patella so that it skimmed its way into the gloom like a coin.

"The will to accomplish your own freedom. Your freedom to be Kings . . ." said the Boy. "Ah, it will stand you in good stead, gentlemen."

"What will?" said the Goat.

"Why, your beauty of course."

There was a long silence during which the two beasts looked narrowly at the Boy, a nasty light in their eyes.

The Boy stood up.

"Yes, you are very beautiful," he said again. "Look at your arms: brindled and long as oars. Look at your sloping back. It is like a storm, mounting as it rises. Look at your shaven jaws as strong as death—and your long muzzle—oh, gentlemen, are they not seductive? Look at your foaming shirt and your mane of midnight. Look at—"

"Why not look at me?" said the Goat. "What about my yellow eyes?"

"To bloody hell with your yellow eyes," mouthed the Hyena savagely as he turned to the Boy. "What was it you said about 'Kings'?"

"One thing at a time," said the Boy. "You must be patient. This is a day of hope and wild revenge. Do not interrupt me. I am a courier from another world. I bring you golden words.

"Listen!" said the Boy. "Where I come from there is no more fear. But there is a roaring and a bellowing and a cracking of bones. And sometimes there is silence when, lolling on your thrones, your slaves adore you."

The Hyena and the Goat looked over their shoulders at the curtained entrance of the Lamb's sanctum. They were obviously embarrassed. But they were excited also and slavering, though what the Boy meant they could not tell.

"What a place to live in!" said the Boy. "This is a place for worms, not for the sons of man. But even the worms and the bats and the spiders avoid this place. For this is a home for fawners, slaves and sycophants. Let it be somewhere free, somewhere splendid, somewhere where you, sir"—he turned to the Goat—"can bury your splendid head in soft white dust, and where you"—he turned to the Hyena—"can cut a cudgel, yes, and use it too. And ah! the marrow-bones for your fierce jaws—the endless marrow! And I have come to fetch you."

Again the two excited beasts looked over their shoulders to where the Lamb sat like a white carving beyond the curtains, save for the dull veil across his eyes.

But the habits of many years are not so easily broken, and it was not until the Boy had gone into detail in regard to where he proposed to take them, and where they would live, and the shape of their golden thrones, and the number of their slaves and a hundred other things that they dared to mention the Lamb: and then it was only because the Boy, unknown to them, had trapped them into a confession of fear. He had not given them a minute to recover, but had jogged their minds along from statement to statement, from question to question, until quite apart from impressing them with his rhetoric he awoke in their bodies the ulcer of insurrection— for they had both been badly scared by the Lamb from time to time and it was only terror held them back.

"Gentlemen," said the Boy. "You can help me and I can help you. I can give you power in the light of the sun. I can give you deserts and green places. I can give you back what once was yours before he tampered with your very birthright. As for what you can give me. Shall I tell you?"

The Hyena came forward to the Boy with something more horrible than ever about the slope of his back. When he was very close he brought his long, shaven head close to the Boy's who could see his own reflection in the beast's left eye, and he saw that he was shaking with fear.

"What is it we can give you?" mouthed the Hyena—and then, quick as an echo—"What is it, dear?" said the Goat. "Do tell your—"

He never finished his sentence, for the air became filled with the voice of the Lamb and as all three listeners turned their heads in the direction of the curtains they saw them part and something trotted out from between them—something unnaturally white.

The long bleat had brought the bristles up vertically on the back and arms of the Hyena, and the Goat had become frozen where it stood. Something had been apprehended in that seemingly innocent note—something which held no significance for the Boy, for he had no experience of the pain that always followed. But for Goat and Hyena it was otherwise. They had their memories. They knew of it.

But one thing that the Boy *did* realize, and that was that the two beasts, being filled with the slime of abject terror, were of no use to him at all, but equally they were no use to their master.

The Boy was not to know that the anger at the heart of the bleat had been awakened by the empty table. Where was the Feast? The feast during which he had hoped to begin his conquest of the wholly human youth. Where were his abominable henchmen?

As he, the Lamb, came through the curtain with his head held very high and his body sparkling like frost he was at the same time listening with his ears cocked, his nostrils dilated, and at once came upon the scent of the Hyena.

Walking with the nimbleness and delicacy of a dancer, the White Lamb came rapidly upon them.

It was now or never for the Boy. Without thinking, he pulled off his shoes and slid soundlessly into the adjacent gloom; to do this he was forced to elbow his way past Hyena and as he did this he saw that creature's knife, a long, thin, deadly yard of steel, and he plucked it from the belt of the beast, and the noise this made turned the blind gaze of the White Lamb full upon him.

In spite of his tip-toeing, not only out of focus but out of alignment with the veiled eye, yet the Lamb followed with a horrible precision the movements of the Boy. Then all at once he turned his long woollen head away and a moment later had followed the path of his blind gaze and was circling the two half-beasts with a kind of strutting action; and as he did this the two creatures collapsed into a kind of decay. They were already travesties of life, but now they were nothing more than the relics of that travesty.

For, as the Lamb minced about them, they gave themselves up to his superior will, their eyes yearning for annihilation.

"When I kiss you," said the Lamb in the sweetest voice in the world, "then you will not die. Death is too gentle: death is too enviable: death is too generous. What I will give you is *pain*. For you have spoken to the Boy—and he was mine from the first word. You have touched him, and he was mine from the first touch. You have spoken of me: and in the hearing of the Boy, and that is treachery. You have not prepared the Feast. So I will give you Pain. Come and be kissed, that the pain may begin. Come to me . . . come."

At the sight of the two creatures heaving their collapsed bodies across the floor the Boy retched with a nausea of the soul and body and, lifting the sword above his head, he moved inch by inch towards the Lamb.

But he had progressed no further than a few feet before the Lamb ceased in its weavings and turning his head to one side took up an attitude of extreme concentration. The Boy, holding his breath, heard nothing in the hollow silence, but the Lamb could hear the beating of four hearts. It was towards the sound of one of the hearts, the heart of the Boy, that the Lamb now directed his entire sentience.

"Do not think there is anything you can *do*," came the voice, like a chime of little bells, "for already you are losing your strength . . . your nature is drifting from you . . . you are becoming mine."

"No!" shouted the Boy. "No! No! you tinkling devil!"

"Your shouting will not help you," said the Lamb. "My empire is hollow and empty, so do not shout. Look, instead, at your arm."

Dragging his eyes away from the dazzling ghoul, he screamed to find that his fingers were not only curled unnaturally, but that the whole arm was swinging to and fro, as though it had nothing to do with him or his body.

He tried to raise the hand but nothing happened, except that as he cried with fear there was a note in his voice he did not recognize.

The concentration of the blind gaze upon him was like the pressure of a great weight. He tried to retreat but his legs would not obey him. Yet his head was free and clear, and he knew that there was only one thing to do and that was to break the spell of scrutiny by some unexpected occurrence, and as this idea flashed through his mind he bent down very silently and placed the sword on the stone floor; and feeling in his pocket with his right hand he felt for a coin or a key.

Luckily there were several coins, and taking a couple he lobbed them high in the air. By the time they landed on the floor beyond the Lamb the Boy had snatched up the sword with his one healthy hand.

Down came the coin with a sudden clang immediately *behind* the Lamb, and for the merest momentary flash of time the intense scrutiny of the tyrant was broken, and a deadly weight of oppression fled out of the air.

This was the only moment: the moment when all must be done before the resurge of evil. The clearing of the air brought with it for one split second the loosening of the adhesions in his legs and a vibrance to his foul left arm so that he sprang forward with no sense of being retarded. In fact the air seemed to open up for him as he sprang, his sword brandished. He brought it down across the skull of the Lamb so that it split the head into two pieces which fell down on either side. There was no blood, nor anything to be seen in the nature of a brain.

The Boy then slashed at the woollen body, and at the arms, but it was the same as it had been with the head, a complete emptiness devoid of bones and organs. The wool lay everywhere in dazzling curls.

The Boy sank to his knees, the relics of the white beast spread about him as though he had been shearing a sheep rather than slaying one.

Out of the intense darkness where Hyena and the Goat had crouched in subjection before their lord, two ancient men emerged. One had a sloping back, the other a sidelong shuffle. They did not talk to one another: they did not talk to the Boy, nor he to them. They led the way along cold galleries; through arches and up the throats of shafts until, in the upper air, they parted without a word.

The Boy was lost for a long while but, walking in a kind of dream, came eventually to the banks of a wide river where innumerable hounds awaited him. He boarded a little boat and was pushed across the water by the swimming pack, and by the time the boat touched ground on the far side his adventure had melted from his mind.

It was not long before one of a host of searchers found him lost and weary in a crumbling courtyard and carried him back to his immemorial home.

NOTABLE SELECTIONS
FROM THE PUBLISHER OF
THE BEST SCIENCE FICTION
IN THE WORLD